A Doctor's Visit

3 Novellas and 5 Short Stories

Also by Siegfried Kra, M.D.,FACP

A Doctor's Visit

3 Novellas and 5 Short Stories

Siegfried Kra, M.D.

LORENZO PRESS

Interior design and typesetting by Swordsmith Productions

FIRST EDITION, First Printing

ISBN 0-9645-2264-0
Library of Congress Control Number:2004100818
www.lorenzopress.com

Printed in the U.S.A.

The author wishes to thank his editor and publisher, Anthony Maulucci, and his agent, Don Gastwirth, for all their brilliant efforts and faith in him.

Dedicated to Lolita, Lisette, and Annice

Contents

Falling in Love Again

WHEN WE ARRIVED in America in 1939 from Danzig, we lived in a small apartment on 99th Street in New York. Each day was a lesson in survival which I have never forgotten. My father, once an important industrialist, was now reduced to shoveling snow off the streets in the winter time to earn a few dollars for our food.

In the basement of our rooming house was a small store that pressed and cleaned suits and shirts. The owner, a tall, fat, ugly man, ran a thriving business. He had a son called Meurice who, after school, delivered the shirts and pants to the neighborhood customers.

One cold day in December, when I was standing in front of the house, I met Meurice who was carrying suits and bundles of packaged shirts from his father's store.

He sized me up and looked at me curiously because I was wearing leather short pants, lederhosen, on such a cold day.

"Why don't you wear long pants?" he asked me. Two months in America and I had a bare knowledge of English. I did not understand a word he said. I just smiled and he became angry.

"Do you want a punch in your face?" he asked me. I understood that as he raised a fist at me in annoyance. Just at that moment his father emerged from the cellar of his store wearing a stained polo shirt, a cigar stuck in his mouth, reeking from sweat and alcohol.

"Meurice," he yelled, "deliver those pants, damn you. He is a greenhorn. He doesn't know any English." Meurice must have felt badly because he signaled me with his hand to accompany him on his delivery.

I followed behind him to the large apartment building on the corner of West End Avenue, through the servants' entrance, up the service elevator to the twelfth floor. He rang the bell. A black woman dressed in a white uniform answered the door. She took the packages, paid the bill and gave Meurice twenty-five cents for a tip.

"See how easy it is," he said, and showed me the quarter in the palm of his hand.

The following afternoon, after school, I waited for Meurice in front of his store. When he arrived, he was carrying a pair of long pants on a hanger.

"Here, this is for you. They are the same size as mine. Someone never came to pick them up."

He took me down to his father's store for a fitting. His father was standing over a large pressing machine, a bottle of beer on the counter. The small room was suffused with the smell of alcohol and smoke as he took a swallow from the bottle, held it in his mouth, and then sprayed the beer on the pants on his pressing board. With one quick thrust, he slammed the large steam board onto the pants and he was surrounded by a cloud of smoke and beer fumes.

The pants were a perfect fit. Meurice and I became good friends thereafter.

"My father will pay twenty-five cents for each delivery," he said. "It is Christmas time and we need help."

I was too young then to notice that Meurice was different from the other boys I knew. He was fair in appearance, slender, and his movements were not like the other boys. He never played curb ball, and was quite shy and kept to himself most of the time. He hated baseball, and was not interested in any of the radio programs I learned to love. It did not take long for me to become Americanized and become a fan of *The Shadow, Captain Midnight, The Green-Hornet, The Lone Ranger* and all the other marvelous radio characters.

As the years passed, Meurice quit high school and moved to Greenwich Village with a friend he'd met at school.

The war ended and another war started. Meurice occasionally came to visit his father who still ran his sweat shop. I continued to live in the same neighborhood and Meurice came by to visit me. He was now tall, handsome, slim, and was unashamed regarding his sexual preference. He worked as a stage set helper in a theatre in the Village and was rejected from military service. Meurice, as a child, had feminine features and appeared fragile. Now, being tall and slim, he looked like a pale weed that a strong wind could break in half.

Twenty years had passed and I was practicing medicine, writing books, and once, after being interviewed on *The Phil Regis Show,* I received a strange phone call. It was an effeminate voice and it sounded desperate. "This is Meurice. Remember me?"

"Of course I do. What are you doing these days?"

"I saw you on the Regis show and I want to tell you, you were terrific."

"Nice to hear from you."

"I have to see you. I have a medical problem that no one seems to be able to solve. Would you take me on as a patient?"

"Call my office, Meurice, and I will be glad to see you."

Ominous words: "I have a problem that no one can solve." I have heard them so many times in practice. It usually means the patient has wandered from doctor to doctor, hundreds of tests have been performed, and there is an underlying psychiatric problem. Once in a while there is a hidden ailment that has not reared its ugly head.

Meurice had not aged one day. His pale baby face did not have one wrinkle and he did not look ill.

"You look the same," he told me, "except your hair is gray, which makes you look more distinguished, like a real doctor should. You have the same strong eyes that I remember." And he suddenly burst out laughing.

"What's so funny, Meurice?"

"I just remembered how we went to the World's Fair in 1939 and we took one of those little car rails and you found a wallet on the seat and inside was fifteen dollars. We came with two dollars each and now we were rich."

"We should have given the wallet to the guard," I told Meurice.

"Well, we didn't and we went to see everything, including the girly show, the Billy Rose Aquacade, the Streets of Paris, and the parachute jump, and you had your first ice cream soda. Now I am here for professional reasons, so I'll get right to the point. For many years I have always felt weaker than most people. I become dizzy and feel weak when I stand too long, especially in a warm room, and now I have had five or more fainting spells, and I am losing weight. I have seen many doctors and they find nothing wrong with me except that my blood pressure is low, which I am told is a good sign."

"Have you had a test for AIDS?" I asked Meurice without much hesitation.

"Believe it or not, I have been with, at most, three men in twenty years, and now I have been living with the same guy for almost ten. We both tested negative. I have had three AIDS tests in the past year, all of which were negative, so I know it is not AIDS. I have had an EEG, brain scans, and all the doctors concluded that it was low pressure which makes me feel weak and faint. I have pills to raise my pressure and I wear a girdle, not because of sex preference but because it keeps the blood from going into my legs."

Nature had played a mean trick on Meurice. When he stood naked in front of me in the examining room, his skin was pale, soft, and he could have easily passed for a woman. The body hair was scanty, and I could not find anything from the examination to account for fainting spells, or "swooning like a Victorian maiden" as Meurice so aptly put it.

As I was making my notes in the chart, Meurice was getting dressed and he suddenly swayed like a drunken sailor and fell back on the examining table. His blood pressure was normal, yet he lay unconscious on the table. His ECG was normal and by the time the ambulance arrived, Meurice awoke.

"I am not going into the hospital because they never find anything wrong with me. It is a waste of money," he said.

As he lay on the examining table, I listened to his heart again. The beat was regular and there were no murmurs.

"Well, you are probably right, Meurice, but a few days in the hospital would be worthwhile so we can observe you and, perhaps, do some more tests and repeat some of the others."

"No, I will not have a hundred needle sticks and curious doctors pawing at me."

"But, according to the records you brought with you, you have not been studied in a hospital like Yale, a university hospital where someone might have a clue to your mysterious story."

"No, thank you."

The ambulance, by now, had left and I resigned myself that I could not help Meurice.

"Just one more question, Meurice," I said. "Are these spells always the same? What I mean is, do they happen usually after you have been sitting for awhile and then stand up?"

"Yes, usually. Sometimes they happen after standing a long time."

"Lie down again, Meurice," I told him. I took his blood pressure again and it was normal. Ten minutes later he stood up, and his blood pressure did not drop significantly, but his face became pale.

"Are you sure there are no other things that are different from before?"

"Well, my joints are always aching," he said, "and I am so tired all the time. Just climbing the stairs exhausts me, and my breath is a little shorter than it used to be."

His chest x-ray was normal and Meurice did not smoke or drink.

"I'd better sit down," he said, "before I go off again."

"Just wait one second more, Meurice. I just want to listen to your heart again."

I placed the stethoscope on his hairless chest and I was surprised to hear a new sound in his heart. It was not a murmur, but it sounded like a bag of sand that had fallen to the ground, a plop-like sound with each heart beat. He lay back on the table and the sound was not there. As soon as he sat up, it was not there. But when he stood up, I heard it again—

a strange, far-away sound, as if I was in an old house and it came from down in the cellar. I was certain I had discovered the mystery of my swooning friend.

It was just about at that time that I was involved in a new procedure called echocardiography. It is a method for picturing the heart through sound waves. In 1970 the procedure was still in its infancy and we used very primitive instruments, polaroid pictures, and we were not certain what we were seeing.

Meurice was suffering from a rare tumor of the heart called a myxoma, which grows slowly and, when it reaches a certain size, impedes the flow of blood through the heart and sends out a sound like a plop heard only when the person changes position.

"I know the diagnosis, Meurice, but it won't be easy to prove." My crude echogram did show something abnormal in the heart.

"Meurice, you will have to come into the hospital and allow me to arrange for a angiogram of your heart, an x-ray, which we can do through a heart catherization."

It took a great deal of cajoling, but Meurice did agree and a myxoma of the heart was found. The tumor was removed, Meurice's fainting spells vanished, and he is now living in Paris doing what he always dreamed of—he has become a female impersonator. Before his surgery he had been unable to stand up long enough without fainting. But now he has become a perfect Marlene Deitrich and we saw him in a little bistro in Paris singing "Falling In Love Again."

A Nun's Story

THE MORNING BEFORE I left New England with my wife and two children for a winter holiday in St. Thomas, Sister M. pulled me aside in the corridor of the Catholic hospital as I was conducting rounds.

"I hear you are going for some weeks to the Islands. How nice," she said.

Sister M. was a tall, stunningly attractive woman with a persuasive way about her. I have always liked her and she me. She was the principal of one of the Catholic schools and also assistant to the director of the hospital. She ran both the hospital and school with an iron hand. "Cleanliness is godliness" was her motto. Infection rates were low, and the patients' rooms and bathrooms were spotless. The nuns as well as the nursing staff kept the patients groomed and washed before the doctors made their morning rounds.

"We have a school on the island high up on a hill. You could do us a big favor," she continued. "Would you mind just visiting our teachers and sort of seeing if all is well?"

I agreed, and we parted amiably.

The next morning my family and I left on our vacation. St. Thomas is a beautiful jewel of an island rimmed by volcanic mountains and surrounded by the blue Caribbean, which changes color from deep blue to turquoise to sparkling emerald green. We arrived without incident and checked into one of dozens of look-alike brown wooden condominiums facing the sea.

Our first day was spent settling in. The following day I rented a jeep and, after studying the map of the Island, headed for the Catholic church up in the mountains where the bustling sounds of the city, Charlotte Amalia, were barely audible.

It was delightfully warm at nine o'clock in the morning. The sky looked like a blue painted ceiling, and the air was filled with the sweet odor of gardenias. Dressed in khaki shorts and white short sleeve shirt, white shoes, a panama hat, with stethoscope dangling from my back pocket, I felt like doctor Schweitzer in Gabon as I drove my jeep up the twisting mountain road. The natives were walking to work from their small wooden homes, each of which had a painted red roof top. The story told by the natives is that when the Danes owned the island they ran out of paint and the mother country shipped hundreds of gallons of red paint only. For hundreds of years the folks on this Island continued the tradition of painting roofs red. The multicolored houses, perched on the edge of the mountain, appeared as if they all would tumble into the sea.

The stone Catholic church, painted all white, stood majestically high on a ridge, facing the Caribbean sea. The Danish Consulate sat adjacent, and the red and white Danish flag flying from the roof of this splendid estate remained as a symbol of another time.

Sweet gentle sounds of church bells tolling the hour echoed through the mountains reminiscent for me of the Valais mountains in Switzerland where I went to school. A moment later I saw a high wrought iron fence that surrounded church property. Standing adjacent to the serene white cathedral was a sinister-looking dark-brown building which I assumed was the convent. On the spacious manicured lawn five young women in swim suits were sunning themselves on tanned-colored blankets. I was a bit startled by the sight of the women sunbathing on the groomed front lawn of the convent.

As I approached, I was greeted by two large German shepherds who ran up to gate barking viciously at me. Keeping a safe distance, I yelled with what I hoped was a strong convincing voice, "Hello, I am the doctor from home and I bring greetings from Sister." The young women ignored me and did not make any attempt to cover themselves. Rather than disturb this secluded world, I decided it made perfect sense to leave it unperturbed and return to my pleasurable new life of leisure and relaxation. But just then, as I was walking back to my jeep, I heard a pleasant voice calling to me. "Welcome to St. Mary School, Doctor." I turned around and saw a young woman standing at the gate smiling at me. She bore a strong resemblance to Sister M. from home. This could not be the woman I had talked to just two days ago at the hospital, I thought.

"Sister M.?" I asked as I approached the gate.

"Yes, Doctor, it's me."

Seeing her there dressed in comfortable island clothing, I was taken back. In her late thirties, she was at least ten years older than the sunbathing teachers on the lawn, but far more attractive. She had the same provocative smile and elegant presence of Ingrid Bergman in *The Nun's Story*. My stare seemed to make her uncomfortable and she moved her hands to rearrange her skirt and said, "Well, dear doctor, how nice of you to visit us. You look surprised to see me. Well, I decided I needed a little vacation. I apologize for the dogs, but we are isolated here." I was about to say, It is wise to have all protection you can muster with those lovely young women lying about on their golden colored blankets as if they were at St. Tropez on the Riviera, but stopped myself. "You could not have come at a more opportune time. One of our senior sisters is very ill and is running a fever."

Sister M. opened the gate. The overzealous dogs retreated as she patted them on their furry heads, but they continued to glare suspiciously at me.

"Just follow me, Doctor. Have no fears, these dogs are very obedient, and sense if someone is not a friend. Sister Louise is upstairs in her bed," she continued.

We climbed the narrow stairs to the third floor. In the hallway lit only by a small ceiling lamp I could hardly see the numbered oak doors. What a striking contrast between the sepulchral scene here and the one outside in the blazing sun.

Sister Louise was covered with several tattered army blankets pulled up to her head of disheveled gray hair. Her pale sickly face stared at me. After Sister M. introduced me, the old woman said, "We are blessed," in a soft mousy voice. She withdrew a wrinkled hand from under the blankets to shake my hand.

In my light summer clothes, I felt nearly naked beside these women covered up in their habits. Short pants and polo shirt was not my usual dress when examining a patient, but it did not seem to bother the nuns. "How do you feel, Sister?" I asked as I sat down on the bed next to her and felt her racing pulse.

"I am so cold and I can't stop shivering," she replied. "What a devoted doctor you are to come my aid."

After I examined her lungs with Sister M. standing by, I was certain she was suffering from pneumonia. Back home I would have sent her straight to the hospital, but she refused to go to the local one, which had a reputation of substandard care.

The sisters, however, were very resourceful. Their medicine chest was stacked with all the medications most hospitals have on hand. The old nun offered me a glass of lemonade which I gladly accepted, although I would have preferred a rum and coke. I gave instructions on how to care for the patient as I drank the lemonade. When I was done I said goodbye and found my own way back outside.

It was good to feel the hot sun and fresh breezes of the Islands again after departing from the sick bed of a pneumonia patient. However, the experience did make me feel like a medical doctor, not a hospital staff member surrounded by troops of interns, residents, laboratories and x-ray equipment, but a real physician using my stethoscope and knowledge I learned during my training years about how to diagnose pneumonia.

The year was 1970, and prior to this I'd held the traditional image of nuns clothed to the neck in either black or white habits, but as I drove down the mountain I kept picturing all those sisters, who were teachers in the Catholic school, lounging almost naked on the lawn. I must admit it was a brief erotic experience that reminded me of what was described in the volumes of Marquis de Sade.

Back at Cowpet Bay my family was preparing for a day of

sailing. My wife was used to these interruptions, either in the middle of the night or even on airplane when a medical emergency arose. "I am glad you don't have your beeper like last time," she said. "Remember when we were on the Gross's yacht in Magen Bay and the coast guard came racing after us?" I recalled how the officer had signaled us to drop anchor so they could board us. We had thought it was a drug search and our innocent rich Cuban host remained very quiet. We thought he was carrying contraband for Castro. Their loud speaker bellowed, "Is there a Doctor Greene on board?" "They're after you," my wife had said. Our host looked worried and we later learned he had been carrying something illegal aboard. My wife continued, "I found the entire situation amusing and welcomed the tall elegant coast guard officer who saluted me and our host. I remember he said, 'We have an emergency call from your friend, Dr. Ladi from Yale New Haven Hospital. Come aboard, sir, and we can contact the Doctor. He said it is urgent he speaks to you now.' " I had never been aboard a coast guard cutter and I was led into the radio room where some officers were drinking coffee. One of them handed me the phone. "Saul, what in the world can be so urgent?" I had yelled. "Are you sick?" "Sorry, about this, my mother is your patient and the Yale people want to do an emergency arteriogram of the pulmonary arteries, and there is a twenty percent risk of dying, you used to tell me.' Why the arteriogam?' I had asked Dr. Ladi who was a generalist. 'They feel strongly it is a massive pulmonary embolism and she is critical and then they want to perform an embolectoy.' "It won't happen," I had said without much conviction. I told him it was the right thing to do and wished him good luck.

"Now what did you do?" my wife asked playfully.

"It's not the coast guard this time," I replied. "It's an old nun at the convent of St. Mary's. She has pneumonia."

A glorious and scary day followed. I took my wife and two daughters sailing, which was uneventful until suddenly the sky darkened and a sharp wind billowed our sails. I tried not to show my panic as we were in danger of capsizing, far from shore. After I pulled the sails down we were out of danger. Once the gale subsided, I raised them again. We arrived safely back in Cowpet Bay and my wife said, "Thank you, whoever is up there." She turned to me and remarked, "Perhaps the nuns prayed for our safety."

That night, still shaken from our sailing adventure, we had dinner at a restaurant called Craig and Sally's with a large wine cellar and the best red snapper on the island. We went to bed early and I was dreaming about sailing with the young nuns in their bathing suits swimming along side us like dolphins and then the gale and Sister M pulling our boat safely to the shore. The phone rang and I awoke abruptly.

"Even on vacation," my wife said solemnly. "You poor guy."

For a instant I thought I was back home. I placed a pillow over my head and ignored the phone, but it would not stop ringing.

"Darling, answer the damn phone so we can all get some sleep," my wife said.

I picked it up and heard the by-now familiar voice of Sister M. "Doctor, I know this is terrible to awaken you at four in the morning. God forgive me, but my heart is racing so fast. It started a while ago and here on the island we have no way to get to the hospital at this hour. What should do?" I learned long ago you don't ignore a rapid heart and a frightened patient. I reassured her and hung up.

"I have to go, dear," I told my wife as I got out of bed. "One of the sisters at the convent is having palpitations."

"What did the convent do before you came here?" my wife wondered. "You should have never told them you were on the island."

The night on this delightful island can bring a smile and a sigh to the coldest heart. The trade winds that brought Columbus to this part of the world blow a soft breeze from the East. The darkness of the night is lit up by a mysterious moon complementing the sparkling stars. You can clearly see Venus glowing and the Big Dipper and the North Star. Pollution from the hundreds of cruise ships had not yet blanketed this magnificent night sky.

On the mountain I beheld a wondrous view. The roads were lit up by the silver moonlight and below the city lights looked like Fifth Avenue at Christmastime. I had never made a house call surrounded by such radiance and mystery. In fact, I had never made a house call to a church to render medical care to a nun at four in the morning.

The dogs were howling, baying to the moon as I drove up to the pale church. The convent had some of the interior lights lit which created an eerie scene. Two of the teachers were waiting for me at the gate, this time wearing blue woolen robes.

"Thank God you came," the younger sister said. The two sisters led me into the convent, up the narrow stairs to a darkened hallway and then to a room numbered one. They opened the door and I went in. Sister M. was lying in the small narrow bed looking pale and sullen. She looked at me with fear in her beautiful eyes. The sick room was sparse with a large cross hanging over the head of the bed. The walls were painted white, a simple two-drawer pine wood night table was next to the bed with a candle and a Bible. An old-fashioned porcelain bed pan was sticking out of the bottom shelf of the night stand.

Three nuns were standing watch like guardian angels. I felt like I had entered a time warp: here I was in the middle of the night standing over a beautiful woman in a setting from another century. If it were from another time, I would probably be wearing a black morning coat with a stiff white collar, and my stethoscope would be a wooden tube, and I would be pulling the porcelain bedpan out of the lower shelf to examine the urine.

Sister M. looked up at me and spoke softly. "My heart is racing. I am not prepared to meet my maker yet. Should I call the priest to give me last rites?" she asked. I sat down on the bed next to her and took her hand, which was surprisingly muscular and felt like the hand of a laborer instead of a young woman. But of course these sisters do men's work. I felt her pulse which was rapid, but regular. "Not yet, Sister M., let me first use my stethoscope. Will one of you ladies be good enough to help sister off with her clothing so I can I listen to her heart?"

I stepped out of the room and waited until I was called back in. They had covered her small bosom with a towel and scrutinized me as I moved the stethoscope around her chest, moving the towel aside. As was my habit, I closed my eyes to hear better. (One famous cardiologist, Paul Dudley White, taught me that music and heart sounds are best with the eyes closed—it sharpens the perception and concentration on the sounds.) My closed eyes might have made Sister M. more comfortable and reassured the other nuns. Sister M.'s heart was indeed racing but I heard no murmurs.

"By the way, you wouldn't have a ECG machine around, would you?" I asked in a skeptical tone.

"We do, Doctor," Sister M. said, covering herself with the

towel. One of the sisters brought it in and attached the straps to her arms and legs and placed the metal chest leads on her bare chest as Sister M. kept repeating how grateful she was that I had come to her aid.

"We were shown how to run the ECG machine, but not how to read it," one of the nuns said when they saw the astonished look on my face. "We have all kinds of heart medications here if you want to use them and we can setup an I.V. We even have a defibrillator," another nun added.

I studied the ECG and announced, "It is just a fast heart beat, Sister, not to worry. If in your little pharmacy you have some Valium, that is all that's needed, and as the sun rises you will be back to normal," I said. "If not call me again. Just wondering, was there anything to upset you, Sister, stress, or anything at all?"

"No, Doctor, nothing that I can think of at the moment— thank you for asking," she replied in a not-too-convincing voice. "Bless you, Doctor, for your kindness and expertise." She sat up and the towel dropped from her chest, and again I had a glimpse of her small breasts. I looked away as the younger nun swiftly covered her once more.

As I was leaving, Sister M. told me the older nun with pneumonia had fully recovered and was asleep otherwise she would have greeted me. I nodded and said good-bye to the three nuns standing by her bedside.

The sun just appeared over the horizon as I left the convent and headed back to Cowpet Bay. Shadows filled the valley below. It was five thirty in the morning and my wife and children were still asleep when I climbed into bed.

At breakfast the phone rang and it was Sister M. thanking my wife for "letting me borrow your husband" and apologizing for disturbing us.

"What a sweet, charming voice that nun has," my wife said when she hung up the phone. "The medication helped her, the heart palpitation disappeared, the sister wanted to tell you."

One week later, two days before leaving our paradise island, my family and I were tanned and rested, but we had no desire to return to the cold gray skies of New England. We made plans to take a day trip to St. John—an island off the coast to be reached by a twenty-minute ferry ride—to do some snorkeling. As we were leaving our condominium apartment the phone rang and my younger daughter, who had befriended a young lad from New England, was the first to pick it up. "It's not for me," she yelled as she put the receiver down. "There is a woman on the phone who wants to speak to daddy." I dropped all the snorkeling gear at the entrance of the apartment and went to the phone. I had a faint suspicion who was calling. I picked up the receiver, said hello, and heard the unmistakable voice of Sister M. speaking softly.

"I am not calling about me," she swiftly said, "but the bishop of the Virgin Islands heard of the excellent care you rendered to the sisters and to me and he wondered if you would give a quick listen to his heart which he said was skipping. He will be glad to come to your place." "We are leaving the Island in two days, Sister, and at the moment we are off to St. John," I told her. My family by now were outside waiting for me. "Hold on, please." I went out to the jeep. I looked at my wife. "It's the nun again. She wants me to see the bishop of the Virgin Islands for his heart. I feel badly to again be at the beck and call of Sister M. and take time away from you and the children. What should I do?" My wife said, "Go ahead for a few minutes. You will do him a favor. I will explain it to the children. After all, how can you refuse the Bishop? I never realized that the U.S. Virgin Islands had a bishop." I went back inside and told Sister M. I would see the bishop tomorrow. "Thank you so very much, Doctor," she said sweetly.

We left for St. John as planned, snorkeled at Trunk Bay, and on the afternoon of the following day my family vacated the apartment to spend the day at the beach as I waited for the bishop. Sharply at 2:00 p.m. a long black limousine driven by a native man in a chauffeur's uniform arrived at our condominium. Seated in the back with a man dressed in a long black robe was Sister M. She climbed out of the limousine followed by the very tall and pallid bishop, who made a striking appearance. The Sister was wearing her white nun's outfit and her blond hair was pinned back.

The bishop came towards me and proffered a long hand with a large bishop's ring on his third finger. Surely he did not expect me to kiss his ring. Instead, I shook his hand like an old acquaintance.

"Most kind of you, Doctor, to take the time out from your vacation and your family."

"Welcome, your Reverence." I had no idea how to address him.

The last time I had been in the presence of such a tall man of the cloth was when I was a child. I was shivering in short pants on a cold wintry day in Greenport, Brooklyn in front of a Catholic church. I was distributing leaflets announcing the showing of a Polish film starring Jan Kapura, the Polish idol, at the local cinema. Greenport had a large Catholic Polish-speaking population, who had no fondness for Jews, and I was not only shivering from the cold but also out of fear. We had just escaped from the Gestapo to come to America, and my father was a distributor of Polish films. Each Sunday, I dreaded having to stand there in my short pants waiting for the parishioners leaving the morning service. The tall priest frightened me as he stood at the doors of the church, telling me to move further back from the entrance. Now, fifty years later, I was greeting a bishop who was as awesome-looking as the cleric at Greenport.

Sister M. said, "I can assist his reverence for the examination." She gave him a knowing, surreptitious glance.

"I am sure we can manage, Sister." He looked at her gratefully as he spoke, his bass voice resounding like an opera singer. I escorted the bishop into the children's bedroom and asked the usual questions about his heart, while Sister M. sat in the living room. I asked him to remove the layers of clothing leaving his chest bare. My examination found a normal heart, and after we returned to the living room, sister asked if they might have a tall glass of water.

"Why not something more refreshing like a gin and tonic?" I asked courageously.

"Splendid idea, Doctor. I am sure Sister would not object." His eyes gave her a soft stare. "She is welcomed to join us if she wishes."

The Ingrid Bergman smile appeared on her pale face with just a hint of a blush in her cheeks. "Of course it would be refreshing," she said, looking a little flirtatiously first at me and then at the bishop as if asking our permission.

The bishop rose from his chair like a giant bat, and, unbuttoning his flowing black gown, walked towards the sliding door that opened onto the porch. He was struck by the cool breeze and the view of the calm sea with sail boats in the distance. "It is like a painting, a Dufy," he announced. "No wonder Camille Pissarro painted here—he was born in St Thomas. I am certain you knew that already. He was of the Hebrew faith like you, Doctor, as Sister informed me. You must have visited the oldest synagogue under the American flag here in St. Thomas."

"Oh yes, we always try to attend Friday night services," I lied. "It's a marvelous synagogue dating back to the 1840's. There is sand on the floor."

Sister M. stayed near me in the small kitchenette. "Let me help, Doctor. You are very generous and kind to us." I opened the freezer and found the almost full bottle of vodka. She reached above the counter to fetch three glasses. She was a tall woman, and did it effortlessly. I bent down to find the tonic water in the lower cabinets; as I rose up I accidentally touched her body and she did not immediately draw back. Next I pulled out the ice tray and handed it to her. She removed the cubes with her fingertips and placed them in the glasses, smiling as she poured generous quantities of vodka into each one. She carried two glasses to the veranda, and handed one to the bishop. I followed her, and we all sat down on the steel porch chairs.

Drinking vodka with a nun and a bishop was a new experience for me.

By the time we had finished three refills of our glasses, with Sister acting as the hostess, we had discussed the politics of the island and Castro. The bishop rose up from his chair looking as serene as he had before, but Sister now had a red glow to her cheeks. Her voice sounded a pitch higher as I escorted them to the door to leave.

"Sister M.," I said almost in a whisper, "you look like Ingrid Bergman, my favorite actress of all times."

"Thank you, Doctor, that is the nicest compliment I have ever received."

The black chauffeur opened the door of the limousine. "God Bless you and your family, this was one of the nicest afternoons I have spent on this island," said Sister M. in her mellifluous voice as she gave my hand a gentle squeeze. Then she climbed into the back seat of the car beside the bishop and straightened the skirt of her white outfit over her long legs. I thought I caught of glimpse of the bishop taking hold of her hand.

Watching the car drive off, I wondered if the chauffeur was thirsty and wished I had offered him a cool drink—and before I knew it I would have been listening to his heart, I thought.

I was so absorbed in these reflections that I didn't notice my family had returned home. My wife suddenly appeared beside me as the limousine departed. "That nun is a beautiful woman. She reminds me of a movie actress," she remarked.

"Actually, she does look like Ingrid Bergman, now that you mention it," I replied coyly.

Two weeks later, back home in New England, my tan was fading, but not the memory of Sister M. and the bishop's visit. However, I did not run into her again until a few months later at the hospital when she asked if she could see me as soon as possible. I asked her if she could come in the following morning, and she told me that would be fine. She arrived for the appointment wearing her traditional nun's outfit, and sat opposite me in my consultation office, looking pallid, and very serious. Her blue eyes were anxious and frightened. She told me the bishop had come with her and was sitting in the waiting room. I went out to greet him but he had already gone.

When I returned and was seated at my desk, she said, "I have a favor to ask of you." She continued in a whisper,

"Needless to say this is most confidential." She moved her chair closer to the desk and bent her body as if to pray. I sat back in my swivel chair not having the faintest idea what this beautiful nun was going to ask me to do now. Ever since I had returned from St. Thomas, the clergy had been arriving at my office in droves—a large number of nuns and priests were becoming my patients. But professional courtesy was getting out of hand and "God bless you, Doctor" and Novenas can't pay the rent. My work hours became longer and I came home later and later. I had now been in practice for two years, and was just about earning enough income to meet expenses, so I decided that no matter how beguiling her Ingrid Bergman smile I would refuse to accept any more nuns or priests.

"Doctor," she began, then cleared her throat and said, "I am leaving the order. I have given my notice. Don't look so shocked, Doctor. I can't lie to myself and to God. I need one more favor from you. I know it sounds terribly vain, but—you saw my breasts, they are too small, and I want to have them enlarged. Can you please refer me to a plastic surgeon, the best one you know?"

Needless to say I was flabbergasted but kept a poker face. My curiosity was burning to learn what circumstance arose to make her decide to quit being a nun and now to be seeking breast enlargement. But I dared not ask her any questions—it was too awkward and personal. She must have fallen in love, but with whom? Could it be the bishop? I also wondered how a young beautiful woman who could double for Ingrid Bergman would decide, in the first place, to enter the Order. I dared not ask her that either. However, I did ask her how long she had been in the Order.

"Five years and ten days, Doctor." And I could see it on her face that she knew what I wanted to ask but dared not.

"Of course, I would be delighted to refer you to the best plastic surgeon I know." It just happened my friend was a plastic surgeon and new in practice as I was.

She thanked me warmly. I wished her all the best and she gave me her Ingrid Bergman smile as she left my office. That smile haunts me to this day.

When I next saw my friend Marvin, he said Sister M. had been to see him and had made an appointment for an augmentation of her breasts. He wondered where a nun would get $3000 for such a procedure. I told him I had no idea, but remarked that Sister M. was a resourceful woman.

I never saw Sister M. again, but that is not the end of the story.

Nuns and priests continued to come to my office for medical care. One of the nuns who consulted me was the same elderly sister whom I had treated for pneumonia at the convent in St Thomas. Sister Louise arrived one morning feeling distressed and anxious.

"I need something to calm my nerves, Doctor. I took charge of the school after we lost dear Sister M. She left the Order. You probably were not aware of this loss, and now it has become my job, and it is a very difficult job, and Father O'Brien, also your patient, advised me to come see you, to get something to calm me and help me sleep." She paused and gave me a quick appraisal. "I know what I am about to tell you is confidential, but my nerves are so distraught, and you were so kind to me in St. Thomas . . ."

"Certainly, Sister, so please go on," I said, my interest and curiosity mounting.

"And to make matters worse—and no one knows this," she said with a pathetic sigh. "Well, a terrible thing has happened in our convent, Doctor, that has never happened before—" She hesitated and started to speak again, now teary eyed. "Someone has stolen three thousand dollars from the coffers and we are in such poor straits."

The Gardener

WHEN I FIRST met Bill, he was wearing a dark suit, a white button-down shirt, and a blue striped tie. He was a tall pale-faced young man with eyes as black as coal. During the day he was employed by a computer firm, but his real ambition was to be a gardener, to own a landscape business. He read my want ads in the local newspaper.

"I need a gardener, a caretaker, someone to clean up the place, cut the grass, and plant flowers, beautiful flowers," I told him. "I used to take care of the grounds myself, but I got tired of it. My garden never seemed to quite make it."

Knowingly he responded.

He arrived at the end of the day when the sun was about to set, in a Cherokee Jeep driven by a young woman. She was a tall slender-looking woman with long brown hair, her eyes were as dark as two amethysts. Her delicate features were like a gently-carved Grecian goddess. She carried a small book with her, which she never opened. The two, side by side, holding hands, looking like they posed for one of Picasso's blue period paintings.

"I will wait for you until you are finished," I heard her say in a soft gentle voice. She handed him a fruit and a small canteen. "It is very warm. You must drink water if you sweat too much; otherwise you will feel weak."

He kissed her on the lips and proceeded to find his way to the tool shed. She sat in the jeep, in the darkness and patiently waited for him. Bill liked to work until the late evening, unperturbed by the darkness.

"Why work at night, and so late?" I asked him.

"It is cooler and the ground is soft and moist at night, and it makes digging and planting easier."

He wore torn dungarees, a red handkerchief around his forehead, and a polo shirt. He began to look more and more like a gardener each night.

He did a splendid job, this nocturnal gardener of mine. Once when a dangerous thunderstorm arrived, soaking the earth that was dry from weeks of torrid heat, he continued digging, unperturbed that his body was soaked from the rain. His girlfriend sat in the Cherokee Jeep quietly in the darkness, waiting for him to finish his night work.

From my window, I saw him place the garden tools in the shed, raise his head to the sky catching the rain in his opened mouth, and then walk over to the jeep. The young woman wiped his face and his hair with a towel as if he just stepped out of a shower. As he backed out of the driveway, she placed her slender arms around his wet body, her lips on his cheek.

What a strange couple. They hardly spoke, but her eyes were always fastened on him.

He planted flowers that I had never seen before. Soon my garden gleamed with a kaleidoscope of rich colors while he looked on with pride like an artist, who created beauty on a canvas. Each week he presented me with a modest bill, and made more suggestions about how to beautify the grounds.

"You have a charming young friend," I told him. "She is welcome to rest inside. She need not sit out there alone in the dark." "No, she likes to sit in the jeep to listen to the wind and the trees."

Now each day I waited for the gardener to come just to catch a glimpse of her. Every night when they arrived she drove the jeep to the far side of the driveway. Then she gave him a red silk scarf and tied it around his head, adjusting it carefully so it did not cover his eyes.

"You must come during the day sometimes, to see the colors of the garden," I told the young woman. "Your boyfriend did such a splendid job."

"Yes, he does it with love. It is his way. I don't have to see the flowers. I can feel and smell the flowers, especially at night when the fragrance is so much keener—perhaps one day I will." "Are you a student?" I asked. I knew she did not want to speak to me, but I persisted. "You look like an art student or an English major."

"Neither, I work as a receptionist at the place where my boyfriend works," she replied. "I used to go to school," she added proudly, unashamed that now she was a receptionist in the computer company just to be near her lover. I pictured her naked standing in the garden like an Aphrodite.

On one night when the cold and warm air met, a thick fog covered my house. A full moon was reflecting eerie shadows on the garden. It was late, and I surrendered to the night. The lovers were not coming. The fog had not lifted and then the lights of the jeep came streaming through the fog. I was in bed, the window opened in my bedroom as I watched the beautiful scene unfold.

She undressed in the darkness, in the moonlight, and her naked feet danced around the flowers, raising her long slender arms to the moon. I caught a glimpse of her radiant body in the bright shimmering blue light. She became a goddess of the night, and her lover was now at her side; he placed flowers that were picked from his garden in her hair .They never touched, as if she was too scared to be touched by anything human.A cloud circled the moon, the fog returned.When the dance was over and she tip-toed back to his jeep, the gardener followed. The jeep moved out of the driveway leaving a magic behind them that had never been there before.

The scene unnerved me for days, perhaps it was all a dream illusion, perhaps the garden now did have magical power that this strange beautiful woman brought into my life. The garden looked more beautiful than before.

The gardener suddenly stopped coming. Days passed and not one word from him.At first I became annoyed, then anger gave way to melancholy. At least he should have had the decency to call if he no longer wanted to work.

He did not even bother to collect his salary. Each night I waited, skipping any engagement just to sit by the window looking, waiting. Sleepless nights followed one after another. The image of the young woman dancing naked in the garden never left me.

Finally, I relinquished my pride as a disappointed lover, and I made the call. He was at home and he answered the phone in his usual ethereal voice.

"I will be there tomorrow, Doctor, I promise," he said. "I was tied up a little." No apologies, no explanations, it was not important enough for him to give any explanations to the old man.

I expected him to arrive in the early evening, but instead

he arrived along in the middle of the morning of the following day. "Where is your girlfriend?" I asked with consternation
in my voice.

I wanted to tell him how I watched their moonlight
dance, and now the garden had become special, magical, by
her touch, her breath on the flowers.

He must have sensed my disappointment.

"We broke up," was all he said. His face was listless and he
no longer seemed interested in his work.

He came during the day, in the torrid sun, all his movements slowed and the garden lost its magical beauty. He neg-
lected to weed and to water, and before long the garden
looked unattractive, abandoned. I dared not say anything to
him. His eyes were red and swollen as if he no longer slept.

He was moving as if he was walking in a dream, going
through the motions of being alive.

"What happened?" I asked him.

"It just happened. One day she said she no longer wanted me."

She had done her job well, this enchanted sorceress from
another world, and then disappeared. "You are so young and
there are hundreds of women out there for you to meet," I
said with no conviction in my voice.

I understood and shared his pain because I knew that
there's only one real love. I, too, felt his loss.

Several weeks later, I asked him to trim the bushes around
the house. He refused the electric cutter and used an old pair
of garden scissors. He worked at a feverish pace sweating pro-
fusely, snipping as if he were cutting out the pain he felt in his
heart. Always in silence, rounding out all the bushes in perfect
symmetry as a compulsive draftsman, completely oblivious to
throngs of hornets circling his head. He suddenly straight-

ened his bent body, flinching with pain from the dozens of bites. He dropped the scissors, desperately slapping hornets from his face and neck.

"Doctor," he called in a soft, hollow voice, "can I see you for a minute?" I was in my study annoyed to be disturbed, angry at the young man for being, so nonchalant, so indifferent to a lost love affair. Not a word of regret. Did he not miss her as I? Was this just another passing fancy? He did not say a word about her; it was as if she had never existed. No wonder she left him. Casually, nonchalantly I arrived at the porch door.

"Some hornets bit me and I'm allergic to them." He looked frightened and his face was the color of mud. I rushed to the medicine cabinet and found only Benadryl, which he swallowed swiftly.

"How do you feel?"

"Not so good, my lips are swelling, and my mouth feels like it is filled with cotton." Right before my eyes his arms and face became reddened and swelled up as if someone blew up a red balloon. His body swayed like a drunken sailor as I guided him to my car. "We have to hurry, there is not much time."

I drove through traffic lights, beeping the horn, swinging my stethoscope out of the window, so they made way for me as I sped desperately to the emergency room. In the mirror I could see his ashen face.

"How are you? Keep talking," I said to him, as if speaking could help him stay alive.

"I can't breathe, I feel something heavy on my chest, everything is dark now, like someone put a mask over my face."

He fell back, I slammed on the brakes, jumped out of the car, breathed into his mouth and thumped on his chest. The gardener stirred. There was no one there to help. He had had a reaction to hornet bites, and he was close to death. One shot of adrenalin and he would be saved.

What stupidity on my part not to have at least adrenalin in my doctor's bag that lay covered with dust in the trunk of my car. That brown alligator bag given to me the day I started practice was once part of my professional dress. Stuffed with medicines to save lives, now it lay covered with years of disuse, the drugs browned with decay, useless. My, how the practice of my art had changed. Once it was used daily to make house calls: the badge of the doctor was like carrying a flag of peace and trust, so that even in the worst neighborhood we were looked upon with reverence and respect. "There goes the doc, let him be."

If I had called an ambulance it might have taken ten, even fifteen minutes before they found the house. He might have died by his magical garden that he planted so lovingly. Finally, minutes later, we were in the emergency room and I screamed into the hall, a scream of despair.

"I have a dying boy in my car. He was bitten by a swarm of hornets."

They carried him to the special room for patients with cardiac arrest. His face was ashen, his eyes opened. My job was done. Now the young physicians, certainly as young as the gardener, were racing to save him. They must have seen themselves lying on the ground. How swiftly they moved, what expert reflexes, not one motion wasted, as I stood there feeling helpless. This is a job for the young. I was a poor surrogate for the ambulance.

I called his mother who at first did not understand. "Better come to the emergency room at once, things are not going well."

"I don't drive," she said. "I will have to call his friend to take me there."

They arrived like twin sisters through the swinging door. His mother was erect, proud looking. A copy of her son, the same eyes, the same poetical face, even the same color of black hair. The young woman with her, the goddess of the garden, was dressed formally. At first I was not sure if she was the same woman I saw dancing so freely in the moonlight. She carried a book with her, as if she was going to have a long wait ahead. Now she was sitting in the waiting room, her face motionless, not a slight tinge of sadness in her face.

She came as the driver and nothing more. "He knew he was allergic to bees," she finally spoke. "He always carried his insect kit with him, right in his jean pockets. Look for yourself. It is still there. He wanted to die."

Inga

HE WAS RELUCTANT to go directly home. Instead of the short drive from his office, he drove his blue convertible through the city and up the long hill to see the purple glow on the hillside. There was a new tiredness in his body as he stared blankly over the valley below. He was just plain bored with everything—his medical practice, his home life, his friends. Something had to change lest he go mad. And soon.

Outside his spacious home the dogwood were in bloom, and the cherry trees were absolutely marvelous. Spring was all around him, but his soul was cold and dreary. He was drained, bloodless.

A limousine with blue and white markings was departing from his driveway. It had just dropped a passenger at his house. Just seeing something new in the awful sameness stirred him with a little excitement, a hint of life.

Sitting on the corduroy brown couch in the family room was his wife and a young woman.

"There you are, Carl. This is Inga. She arrived a day earlier

34

than expected. You remember the new governess we wrote for? She speaks only German."

The young woman rose from the couch, smiling, small and dainty, hand outstretched.

He had not spoken German for years, but the words came easily, unselfconsciously, as if all those years had never passed.

"Welcome, did you have a good trip?"

"Yes, this was my first time on a plane."

"We must speak English to Inga, dear, because she is here to learn English, and the children will learn German."

"Yes," Inga said softly in German, "I must learn English."

After excusing himself, Carl changed into his work clothing to work on the pool. This summer he decided he would do all the outside work himself, unencumbered by the usual small army of gardeners and pool people. He took the hose, attached one end to the skimmer and lowered the other into the pool with the attached vacuum cleaner. The water was green and dead and murky, much like his own life, he thought. It would take weeks for the pool to clear. In the morning he added gallons of chlorine and other chemicals. He bent down to sense the temperature and for an instant he saw his reflection on the very bottom of the pool. As he rose from his squat position, Inga was standing a few yards away. She wore a brown skirt and a white blouse. She had a quiet-looking narrow face with tepid blue eyes. Her features were more Oriental than Nordic. Her slender neck looked like soft white velvet bedecked by long brown hair.

"It beautiful here." She spoke her few words of English with a charming German accent.

"I hope you will like it here," he said in German.

"Surely I will. I have never been in such a house," she responded in kind.

Later, they were in the family room again and his wife was trying to explain her chores to Inga.

"You will have to tell Inga what her duties are."

Now the words came even easier, and for a moment Carl was transformed to another place, another time, and when he had finished speaking to her, his eyes stared in the distance, to the far past.

Long ago, he had been desperately ill and his parents brought him by train to the hospital in Berlin. Feverish and weak, he rested his head on his governess' lap while she stroked his head and kept a cool cloth on his forehead. He could still smell the sooty smoke of the train as it flowed through the window, and he could hear the nervous cries of his mother. The governess said little and smiled gently, touching his brow with her soft cool hands, which made him feel safe. In the hospital she stayed with him while he was examined and blood was taken from his arm. Then, after he was well, they spent two full days in Berlin at the Park Hotel, his parents in one room and he sharing the other with his Fraulein. The year was 1937.

"You haven't heard one word I said," he wife yelled. "Stop daydreaming. You have to give me some help. I am trying to tell her that every morning you must have your damn squeezed orange juice, and how to prepare it."

He gave Inga an almost imperceptible smile and apologized to his wife. He rose from the couch and poured himself a glass of brandy. Then he translated what his wife was trying to explain to Inga. He looked into Inga's eyes and became very sad.

His wife went briskly into the kitchen, once again

annoyed with his usual indifference.

"You speak German very well," Inga softly said.

"I should. I was raised in Germany."

"Ah, that explains it."

"It has been a long time since I spoke any German. It is a beautiful language."

They sat quietly for a while and then he offered her a cigarette. She hesitated, as if waiting for permission from his wife to smoke. Then she took it. They sat quietly smoking. His daughter entered the room.

"This is Inga, sweetheart. She is from Germany and speaks very little English. She will stay with us for six months to help your mother, and you will learn German."

"Neato," Laura gleamed.

"How do you call yourself?" Inga asked.

"My real name is Gretchen, but everyone calls me by my middle name, Laura."

Laura wore a pair of cut-off jeans and a rumpled white blouse. She sat quickly between them. She was a friendly youngster, thrilled to finally have a friend in the big house. They liked each other right away, and Laura took Inga to show off the house and her room.

The brandy soon had its most desired effect on him and he began to softly hum to himself a song his Fraulein had taught him so long ago, the "Horst Wessel," the Nazi anthem.

Everyone wore a uniform then and sang that song. His father wore a white uniform in the summer and a black one in the winter. His Fraulein spent hours in his large playroom teaching him the difficult gothic script. She sat close to him and took his hand, making him draw the curlicues of the letters on his small graphite blackboard. She read him stories about the Katzenjammer Kids in the evening, and then he had to read out loud to her.

"A gentlemen has to learn to speak the high German, not the low-class one, and you will be an important gentleman someday," she reminded him, feeling pride and pleasure.

The following morning he was at work, but everything seemed different. He bought a German newspaper, the *Aufbau*, and sat reading it at his desk. He now longed to speak German, to eat German food. Everything around him felt strange, foreign. During the day he called his home several times, hoping Inga would answer the phone so he could speak his native language—and hear her voice again.

Several weeks later, making one of these calls home, his wife answered.

"She is impossible. She still doesn't understand more than a word or two, and now I have more work than ever before. It is like having another child. I don't want one. I think we should send her back."

"Well, let's give her a few more weeks," he said weakly. "Laura likes her a lot. Didn't the agency tell you she knew little English? Don't worry, tonight when I get home I will again tell her she must learn English. Let's enroll her in that accelerated language course at the college."

Coming home was no longer a tedious and boring ride. He took the shortest route, daring to travel through the dangerous neighborhood. He was excited, his heart even skipping a beat. He now fully realized that he had been a stranger, a foreigner, disconnected, a displaced person, and that it was Inga who brought him home.

"This is the earliest you've been home in years," his wife said in surprise, as he entered the front door, almost breathless.

"Yes, we are going through a slow period." Ignoring his wife, he glanced through the living room towards the family room, but did not see Inga.

"Where is our second child?" he smirked.

"Inga is downstairs in the basement."

"How about some drinks before dinner?" his wife said. "Now at least I can sit and talk with you for a minute or two."

Inga was now in the kitchen, which was connected to the family room by a door that was slightly ajar. He heard the soft sounds of her movement and for an instant spotted the tight dungarees that outlined her slim body, and the white blouse that so flattered her youth.

"Inga, would you like to join us for drink?" his wife called. He sat back in anticipation, folded his arms, watched the clock on the mantle. Although only a minute passed, it seemed much longer before she finally came softly into the room.

"My wife asked if you would like a drink with us before dinner," he repeated in German.

"Yes, thank you," she said.

He dared not look at her. He was afraid of betraying his joy and excitement.

"I am going to make you a real American drink, a martini."

"Yes, I have heard of martinis."

"They are very strong, so you must drink it slowly."

Inga sat languidly on the easy chair, her slender legs casually apart. From the corner of his eye he watched her take small sips from the small glass while his wife chattered on about the dog show to be held in a few weeks. She was president of the animal shelter and had organized a charity benefit called "Adopt a Dog." When their German shepherd had died a few years ago, his wife decided not to have any more dogs in the house. The loss of their dog was too much to have to bear again. Inga's melancholy and pallid face took on a slight pink hue. Not for a moment did she take her eyes off him. The family room became alive, electrified. The magic was suddenly broken with the ring of the telephone. His wife jumped off the couch to answer the phone in the kitchen.

"I want to see and learn everything in America," Inga said to him in a deep and subdued voice. "I want to see New York."

"And so you shall, you must. New York is for the young. You belong in New York," he whispered back, daring to touch her arm for a second.

When his wife returned she had that look he knew so well. The lips were slightly curved, her eyes had grown smaller—she was upset. Was it that the keen woman sensed the electricity? Did she suspect, instinctively, that her territorial rights were being threatened?

"Mother is ill. That was Adel," his wife said. "I have to go to New York tomorrow. It is good timing that Inga is here. It sounds like Mother is having a stroke, or something."

"I'll go with you," he said, "and then bring her here. I'll put her in the hospital."

"No, I will go and see what the situation is. It's best I go tonight. I won't sleep anyway for worrying. She is almost eighty. And you know my hysterical sister."

"Her mother is sick," he translated in German. "My wife has to go to New York tonight. Perhaps you would like to go with her and you can see a little of the city."

"No, I will stay here."

"I asked Inga if she would like to go with you."

"No. Inga can take care of you and make breakfast. I'll go alone. I'll call as soon as I can."

When they came back from Berlin the bombing had started and they sent him and his Fraulein to Sopot by the Sea. He did not miss his mother. His father wanted him to wear the brown uniform of the Hitler youth.

"Sooner or later you will have to be a member of the Party. Remember I am an officer and it is expected. It is an obligation for you as for me."

The beach was white and crowded and the Fraulein played in the sand with him, building castles and lolling in the warming sun. The heat of the sun on his nearly naked body made him feel so at peace.

After dinner, Carl poured another glass of brandy and smoked a cigarette. He only did that when he was alone and his daughter was asleep. He found the old record of Marlene Dietrich singing, "Do you want to buy an Illusion," and started to play it. He lowered the lights in the family room. With his eyes closed he heard the gentle rustle of Inga's nightgown as she slipped into the room and sat next to him.

"What funny slippers," he laughed as she placed her feet on the couch. They were large, fluffy, red—much too large for her small feet.

"My mother made them for me. She was afraid I would be cold in America. I have a robe to match."

"Some brandy?" he asked her.

"Yes, please. I feel a little chilled after my pine bath."

At night the Fraulein had always worn a nightgown at the beach house, and she too had smelled of pine soap. They played Lotto and listened to the radio until the late hours of the night. Then they went to bed and the Fraulein let him sleep in her bed, against her soft and heaving breast.

He stroked her legs just above her red slippers—he had forgotten how smooth a young woman's legs could feel.

"How old are you anyway?"

"I am going to be 22."

"Any boyfriends?"

"Yes, I have a friend. We lived together in Freiberg, in the Black Forest. That's why I'm here. I wanted to be away for a while."

Her face blushed and she did not want to talk more. They kissed as she curled up against him like a small cat.

"I am going to stay a few days," his wife said during her call in the morning. "Mother is alright, just lonely and frightened. As usual, my crazy sister exaggerated everything. How are Inga and Lori?"

"They are doing well, and Lori wants to sleep over with her friends."

His wife returned several days later.

"You look like you haven't slept at all," she said to him.

"Every night I have been called out." He lied so easily he startled himself.

It is the first lie that is the hardest, he thought, not without some discomfort, and then it becomes easier and easier. After a while the lies begin to sound like the truth, even to the liar, perhaps especially to the liar.

Inga went everywhere with them. They visited Boston and the newly constructed Fanueil Hall Center. Inga became like a sister to Laura. She charmed all their friends with her sweet ways and her soft gentle voice. Sometimes he was able to sneak home at lunchtime when he knew his wife would be away and rejoice in his newfound life. Sometimes Inga came into his study, pretending to dust, and placed her arms around him and gently kissed him. He became less and less cautious as he stole down to her room in the middle of the night, and in the morning she gave him teasing glances. It was delicious.

He made arrangements to attend a medical conference in New York.

"Would you mind taking Inga with you?" his wife asked.

"Of course, I mind. I don't have time to give her a guided tour."

"You don't have to be a tour guide. She will stay with some friends she has from Germany, so you'll be off the hook. Just take her in and then bring her back when you're ready. I did promise her to let her go to New York in December to see all the Christmas decorations."

They stayed at the Regency Hotel and they walked everywhere hand in hand. He showed her F.A.O. Schwartz, and watched her eyes glow like a child's when they went to Rockefeller Center and saw the marvelous window display at Saks Fifth Avenue.

"I want to buy you a fur coat and jewels and diamonds," he told her at Tiffanys.

"I have you," she said. "That is enough," and she kissed him on the cheek as the finely tailored salesman showed them a pearl necklace nestling in its bed of black velvet.

* * *

The Fraulein took him to Berlin to await the arrival of his parents from Marienbaden. They stayed at the Kaiserhof Hotel and shared a large four-poster bed with huge down pillows and covers and had breakfast served in the room. He did not want to eat in the dining room with all the people in uniforms. Each afternoon they went to the zoo across the street from the Reichstag, or down the Tiefengarten, then to Bismark Street, and their driver took them down Gruenwald Forest and through the lake in a small boat. It was chilly in the fall but they didn't mind it. In fact, they hardly noticed it.

"I am the captain of this ship, and you are my prisoner. I am taking you to India forever, away from the war."

"Yes, my brave captain."

"And we are never coming back—never."

"Yes, my brave captain."

When they walked past Rockefeller Center he stopped by the Swiss tourist office. Inga wore a black leather jacket over her silk blouse and leather skirt. There was a late autumn chill in the air and she snuggled close to him as they both stared at the display in the window. It was a poster of the scene in Wengen, with a Swiss valet in the center of the picture and contented cows on a lush hill.

"I want to live in that chalet with you," he said. She squeezed his arms with her long red fingernails and smiled. Her face glowed with love when she looked at him. In the reflection of the window, his gray hair made him feel silly, especially because of the child-like face of Inga. They quickly departed, as if running away from their reality.

On their last night in New York, he took her to the Verdone Restaurant, only a short walk from the hotel. It was a dreary rainy night, but they felt giddy, were indifferent to the rain as they strolled together, huddled under a small umbrella.

On the seasoned headwaiter's face there was a nostalgic look as he served these two unlikely people. Between two other tables, they were completely oblivious of the other people around them. He ordered champagne, smoked a cigarette, and beneath the table, she stroked his leg with her hand.

"I'll love you forever," she whispered to him in German. He felt proud to be with such a young beautiful woman. All around him sat people of his own age. Deliberately, he spoke German with a loud voice to make him appear foreign, as if they were visiting New York for a few days and would soon be on their way back to their homeland.

The champagne got to his head and he talked freely about things he had never said before or admitted to.

"I have been a dead man for too many years. I don't belong anywhere. I have never recovered from being displaced. A stranger of fifty years. Crazy, isn't it? But with you I am home. Nothing seems crazy anymore."

She squeezed his hand and looked at him longingly.

A gruff-looking man smoking a large cigar approached their table, with dispatch and great determination.

"Dr. Braun, what a surprise!" the man almost shouted in his enthusiasm. His wrinkled and tanned wife was beside him, each wrinkle representing the full measure of malice and bitterness in her heart as she eyed the young woman with the young skin.

"Why, Larry and Beatrice, this is my cousin from Germany. Inga."

"A beautiful cousin at that," the man said. He pumped her small delicate hand.

"Yes, I am showing Inga a little of New York."

They exchanged a few more words—pleasantries meant to cover secrets—as he felt his face flush then seem to be burning.

After they left, he was somewhat deflated. "That pompous ass lives a few houses down from ours," he finally said, starting to feel himself again.

Arm in arm, but more tentatively than before, they walked into the luxurious lobby of the hotel, unaware of the man in a dark suit observing them from a corner of the lobby.

Waiting by the elevator, Carl squeezed her hand in anticipation. The man scrutinized the young woman with the leather jacket, short skirt, and high heels.

On the 12th floor, they emerged from the elevator, now intoxicated, giggling and swaying, singing German songs. The man in the dark suit was suddenly there. He stepped in front of them.

"Are you registered in this hotel?" the man asked.

"What business is it to you? Are you the gestapo?" the doctor answered, trying to mask his uneasiness with a belligerent tone.

The man produced a badge.

"Security."

"It is the gestapo!" the doctor said.

"This is my wife and this is my key. How dare you! There will be more to say about this."

"I do apologize. It is my job, you know. Sorry."

At the Kaiserhof Hotel a tall man approached the Fraulein and the boy.

"Is this your son, Fraulein?"

"No, I am the governess. We are waiting for his parents."

"Very well. It is best not to linger in the hotel," the man in the black raincoat said.

Just then, his father, resplendent in his immaculate white formal uniform, appeared with his mother, wearing a long black evening gown that flattered her full figure.

"There is my son, up so late."

"Your son is growing fast," the man in the black uniform said. "Soon he should be in the Youth Group."

The boy blushed and held on tightly to his governess' hand.

In the room he didn't undress, but sat in the chair, thoughtfully, while Inga combed her hair. Was it the champagne that made him feel so confused?

She took out a small brown bottle, and, using a special spoon, he sniffed the white powder into his nose. His nostrils became red, and he felt warm and then they both began to laugh, again fully at ease, the last traces of confusion having evaporated.

"He thought I was a trollop," she said, and sighed. They sat on the richly carpeted floor and she leaned against his chest. He closed his eyes, serene, floating, blissful.

He saw his father in the ballroom standing at attention next to Albert Speer, and everyone applauded as his father was given a prized and revered medal.

"You should be proud of your father," the man in the black raincoat said.

It was raining when they drove up the Hudson Parkway. She sat very close to him, from time to time offering him the tiny spoon with the white powder.

"Why not? It will make the trip back to hell easier," he said aloud, the bitterness in his voice more resigned than angry.

"Thank you for such a wonderful week-end," she said, kissing his unshaven cheek. "I will never forget it. I will love you forever."

Through the leafless forest, the house could be seen from the road. They slowly drove up the circular driveway. Now it all looked barren and foreign to him. Had he been there before?

From then on, each and every day, he maintained his high, never allowing the cocaine to desert his hungry system.

Life continued the same way for him as the winter months stole in, almost unnoticed by him. He no longer complained to his wife about his daily hardships at work, and he became a good and concerned listener to his daughter's crises. And he always knew when Inga was near or had recently left the room because of the small traces left behind—sometimes the stub of a Gauloise cigarette, other times, the crease in the couch which marked where she sat, the smell of pine from her bath, which seemed to linger for hours. Sometimes he spotted her underclothes in the pile of family wash. Sometimes, while putting away his shirts, she slipped something of herself into one of his drawers. At night, when his wife was sound asleep, he crept downstairs to her room where she slept, invariably, like an innocent child. He had only to breathe on her cheek and she surrounded him like a spider, arms and legs embracing and pulling him.

At Christmas-time they had a large tree that Inga decorated, and his wife bought presents for her. The house was filled with joy. Even then they were able to steal wonderful minutes, sometimes as much as an hour or two when the house was empty.

But Inga became irritable as spring approached. She began to avoid him and to ignore his private glances. Instead of staying home when his wife went shopping, she now left the house with her and drew closer to her.

"Is there something wrong, something I did?" he asked her forlornly one day when she happened to be cleaning his room.

"Nothing wrong. I'm just not in the mood now," came the terse reply.

Several weeks later, Inga announced at the dinner table that her boyfriend from Germany was coming to fetch her so they could tour the States. "He will be here in the morning and I must leave."

He looked at her, first with surprise, then shock, then panic.

"Inga is becoming bored here," his wife said nonchalantly. "I agreed she could leave a few months' earlier than planned."

"It is much better, and thank you very much," Inga said.

The bombing never seemed to stop for an instant. He was sent, for safety, to Vacha, with his Fraulein, to a small country house. Also, there they still had fresh eggs and milk every day.

His Fraulein told him, when he was in bed, nestled against her bosom, that his parents were killed in one of the bombings. She pressed him close as the small body stiffened.

"I had instructions to send you to Switzerland to be with your uncle," she said. "I will come to see you in a few months. I promise."

She packed the car and gave him a basket of food for the trip.

"I will see you soon," she promised once more, but he never saw her again.

The following morning Inga's boyfriend arrived with a large well-appointed van. The cabin looked like a bedroom. The boyfriend carried her valises into the van, effortlessly, joyfully.

"Thank you for everything," Inga said, kissing him on the cheek.

When he went back into the house there were valises—familiar pieces—waiting by the front door. A long limousine drove up.

His wife and daughter kissed him. His daughter was crying.

"Where are you going?" he asked, bewildered and fearful.

"We are leaving, too," his wife said, unmistakable disdain in her voice. "Look on the kitchen table. You'll understand."

They left without another word, the daughter still crying, the wife in an obvious hurry.

On the kitchen table one place was set for dinner. There was an open letter on his plate.

Dear Dr. and Mrs. Braun:

We regret the embarrassment we caused you and your wife during your stay at the Regency. Our security guard is guilty of an inexcusable behavior. We wish to make amends by offering you, gratis, of course, our honeymoon suite for a week. Again, we sincerely apologize and look forward to serving you soon.

Sincerely,
The Management

He watched his wife and daughter drive off and walked slowly towards the pool which was still filled with murky water, and now he was sure that he saw himself lying on the bottom.

Death of a Doctor

REVEREND COLLINS WAS at the funeral, along with family, friends, and patients of Dr. Allan Tisherman. The chapel ceremony took 20 minutes, and then the family and closest friends headed for the cemetery outside the city, following the gleaming hearse. The service was brief.

The day was oppressively hot, and I was on the way to my car when Reverend Collins touched my elbow. "Can you spare a few moments from your busy schedule, Doctor? Dr. Tisherman was our family physician for many years. Would you be willing to take my family on?"

"Certainly. I would be honored."

Reverend Collins was the Methodist leader in the community, an important and influential man. Having him as a patient would be a windfall. I knew that many more would follow.

I had been in practice for only some three months, and I was still having severe growing pains. I had a single patient scheduled for the long afternoon.

"Stop by this evening, after your hours," he said, "and I'll give you our files Dr. Tisherman left."

"Oh, I can make it before that. My schedule is rather light today."

"Splendid. Just walk over to the rectory when you're done."

We shook hands and parted. I felt elated, and suddenly remembered that old saw that said, "Every loss contains some gain."

I had met Dr. Tisherman several years ago. I was a resident, he the attending physician. He had blue eyes, dusty hair, and a light complexion. Tall and lean, he was an impressive figure in his white coat. He rarely discussed medicine as such, but chatted easily about everything from books to sailing and the business end of the medical practice.

I met his wife and his children for the first time at the funeral parlor. She politely thanked me for coming to the funeral and asked if I wouldn't mind covering his practice till things got sorted out. I was struck by how businesslike she was, how reserved and even serene.

The rectory was on the main street, and adjacent to it was a typical New England shingled white house built early in the century, an open porch spanning the front. There was a rather small and jarringly unkempt lawn, surrounded by a picket fence missing a few teeth. There was no bell on the door, only a sign which read, "Welcome, please come in."

Reverend Collins was sitting in the living room in his shirt sleeves, wearing his bow tie. He wore reading glasses low on his nose. He rose from the chair at his desk, greeting me warmly.

"I'm sorry for being so late." I had arrived later than I had planned—the phone in my office hadn't stopped ringing.

"I know," he smiled knowingly, "and you'll be even busier shortly. Dr. Tisherman's patients have been calling all afternoon to find a new doctor. Some cold cider, Doctor?"

"I would welcome it."

The living room had two worn easy chairs, and there was a long, equally worn couch. A dark and massive piano dominated the room. Family photographs lined the mantle. There were no paintings, no books, nothing of note to distinguish the room except for a worn Persian, which only made the room even shabbier.

A few minutes later, the Reverend sauntered into the room, balancing a pitcher of cider and two flowered tumblers on a small tray.

"My family is away," he said in a friendly tone, "in Morocco, so I'm a bachelor again for a few weeks. Did you know that my wife is going to be ordained next year?"

I hadn't known.

I sat silently as he served the cider and continued talking, his voice even, monotonous, and soporific.

"Our family, for many generations, has been in the clergy. My son—the family black sheep—didn't want to go into the ministry. He's an intern at the hospital. But then there's Mary. She's at divinity school, and her husband is a minister, which makes up for the prodigal, who's off climbing mountains in the Rockies, or somewhere, this summer. And then there's my brother, Martin, a severe schizophrenic who still lives here with us. My mother is a hale ninety and will be coming to visit in the fall. Our group will keep you pretty busy."

In the corner of the room there was a small desk containing a hurricane lamp, and the Reverend continued his talking as he reached into one of the drawers and brought forth a stack of folders.

"These are our records. All our inner selves."

He handed the folders to me. I glanced at them briefly.

"They certainly seem readable, unlike most doctor's records I've seen."

"Oh, yes, Dr. Tisherman was a quite compulsive man. Everything just right and in perfect order. Nothing out of place."

"How pitiful that he died at the height of his career," I added quickly.

He looked up, his eyes unmoving. "It would have been a tragedy had he lived on," the Reverend said softly.

"Don't look so shocked, young man. Did you know Dr. Tisherman?"

"Only superficially."

"I think I must tell you, then, something about him—in complete confidentiality, of course—since you will be seeing most of his patients, as you have surely already surmised. They are, by and large, good people, rich and solid citizens, the backbone of this congregation." He settled himself into the frayed armchair, his glasses even lower on his nose.

"He had a carriage practice, the best." A brief silence.

"Well, Al Tisherman came to our town eighteen years ago, with his wife. He had just finished his training in New York, and decided not to go back to his home town of Philadelphia. He moved into the house across the street, right off the Green. Mary brought over a cake and we welcomed him. I liked him right away. He was a nice sort of fellow—not more than thirty, I guess—so enthusiastic and determined to do well. He wasted no time at all finding out exactly what to do—what clubs to join, where to be seen, and soon enough he sat on the Board of Education and attended all the Town Hall meetings. I even suggested that he join a temple, but he wouldn't hear of that since he belonged to the Unitarian Church, having long given up Judaism.

"I still remember the first day that we met at our house. Allan was quite brazen—part of his charm, I think. We didn't drink alcohol in our house, so Elizabeth served milk. He asked for a beer.

" 'Why did you pick a small town? You're obviously a city slicker. New York or Philadelphia would be your speed, it seems to me,' I told him.

" 'And Paris,' Allan added. 'I lived in Paris for a year on a scholarship. I wanted to go somewhere where I was really needed. I needed to get away from those crazies of the big cities frantically running their fool heads off. I wanted to raise children amidst oaks and hemlocks and gardens, and in peace and safety, to get to know my neighbors, to feel that I'm part of the community.' "

"Well, you'll get all that here, if it doesn't get too boring for you."

" 'Oh, I'm sure I won't be bored. This is my kind of life.' "

"Well, I asked him if he would like to take care of our family, and we became his first patients. It didn't take long after that for him to really settle in. I mentioned his charm, and he had quite a sense of humor, especially appreciated by the old folks. He had a very special knack with them, like no other doctor I'd ever seen.

"Would you like some more cider, Doctor?" the Reverend asked. "I see a skeptical look in your eyes, or is it puzzlement? One moment I'm telling you Dr. Tisherman is better off dead, the next I'm glorifying him as a saint. Presently, in due time, you be the judge, my dear man.

"Would it be of any interest to tell you that I've seen a great deal of the world from my missionary work in East China? I was a prisoner of the Japanese, spent four years in Vietnam before the French came, and then those three years in the jungle of San Paula. I did all these things as a young man, until, you understand, we decided to have a family. So we settled down here in this little city. I know a little bit of the world, Doctor, and her people, but in all the world I never met anyone quite like Dr. Tisherman."

At that moment, the phone rang. It was for me. The call came from the emergency room and made me feel both disappointed and relieved. I was curious, but exhausted by it all.

"Well, another time," he said. "Soon?"

"Of course."

The town was heavy with humidity as early evening arrived. In the emergency room there was an air of agitation, and tempers were sharp and quick. There was no end to the people who arrived suffering knife wounds, automobile traumas, bad drug trips—as if all humanity were on a massive suicide mission. An air of violence pervaded this once quiet New England oasis. Now, pimps and whores (and those searching for them) walked and drove the streets. The night people had arrived—an endless resource of emergency room care and despair.

"Oh, you aren't Dr. Tisherman," a tiny elderly woman said in a strong, disappointed tone. "He knows my case so well." The poor woman hadn't yet learned that Dr. Tisherman was dead.

"I'm attending to his patients for now," I said gently.

"When will he be back? I have to see him. Can't you get in touch with him and just tell him that Mrs. Cody needs him?

Not that you aren't a good doctor, young man. I'm sure you have a nice kind face. It's just that I've got one of those dizzy spells again. It scares me so, living alone. Don't you see? I need Dr. Tisherman."

She looked so fragile and delicate, so bird-like, her gray hair tied in a small bun, as she lay there in the hospital cart, alone and clearly frightened. It wasn't long after that she began to cry, in small muffled sobs.

"Everything is all right," I told her. "You will be fine." But no matter what I said, it had no impact on her. She understandably wanted her own doctor, who held her in some kind of thrall, a spell of confidence that I hoped one day to achieve with my patients.

"I'll call him first thing in the morning," she said, "and I'll get right over to his office."

And it didn't end there. The next day saw a steady procession of Dr. Tisherman's patients. As the dreary afternoon wore on, each one seemed more devoted to him. Some learned of his sudden demise and were so completely shattered by his death that they couldn't have grieved more if he were a member of their immediate family. His death seemed to wither them.

It was only several days later that I managed to get to Dr. Tisherman's office. There was nothing special in its appearance. The decorations were sparse, his private office was immaculately neat, as if he expected not to return the next day and he knew that someone would be looking into his private life. His receptionist was a woman of thirty, plain in appearance, with strong cat-like eyes that effortlessly pursued me across the office, focusing on my every move.

Each of the patient's charts that I inspected was neat, concise, precisely followed the format learned in medical school. What struck me most about the patients was that none seemed really ill. Other than minor complaints, all of them suffered only from fatigue, some loss of memory, depression, and loneliness. After borrowing some of the charts, I asked if I could also borrow some medications from the doctor's cabinet—some injectables I thought I might need.

"I don't see why not," she said, unpleasantly. "He's certainly not going to need them any longer."

Some of the shelves were stacked with dozens of small brown bottles. They were unlabeled. Further inspection revealed that they contained a white, snowy powder. I was too embarrassed to ask the nurse what they contained, perhaps anxious about displaying my ignorance or just reluctant to intrude. I'd never seen cocaine, except as described in the textbook I used in medical school.

The first patient of the day was a tense elderly man with an impressive almost noble face, who had arrived for his monthly checkup.

"What has Dr. Tisherman been treating you for?" I asked.

"Don't you see it in the chart?" he answered belligerently.

"Not really. It indicates that you are doing fine, and that there are no problems."

"Of course I have problems." He cited a laundry list of symptoms which suggested disorders from the top of his head to the tips of his toes—as if he were quoting a table of contents from a medical text.

"And what does Dr. Tisherman give you for all these complaints?"

"Well, he has his own treatment. He gives me some medications."

"Does he give you the medication in his office?"

"Oh, yes indeed! He inserts the medications into my nose, into each nostril, and that keeps me comfortable for a little while. So, if you don't mind, Doctor, I'd like to have my usual treatment, which is long overdue anyway, I can tell you that much," he said anxiously.

"I don't know what Dr. Tisherman has given you. It doesn't appear on the chart."

"Well, then, you must certainly know. You're a doctor, too. What does one prescribe for these symptoms?"

"Well, see for yourself. You can look at your own chart. What does one prescribe?"

The old man was slender and distinguished, dressed in a comfortable manner, with frayed flannels and an old tweed jacket with the customary leather patch on the elbows. He was 83, had his own teeth, and much to my surprise, didn't wear glasses. I began to read the chart.

"You're 83, the chart says."

"That isn't correct. I'm 93," he said matter of factly. "Dr. Tisherman has given me treatment whenever I need it. He also gives me injections."

I was at a complete loss. Then I remembered the long row of brown bottles with the white powder in them, and suddenly the doctor's magical treatment became all-too clear.

The old man left, disappointed and in anger, and told the receptionist he would find another doctor. I had given him no treatment.

That same evening, I returned to see Reverend Collins who

was sitting at his desk, working over some papers.

"The budget of the church. It gives more headaches than I can care to say. I never was much on pecuniary matters. Nowadays, a minister has to be a good businessman, just like you doctors," he smirked.

"I thought you'd be back tonight. Oh, yes, Dr. Tisherman left his patients quite happy, which, I gather, you've discovered by now. I found out about it one day a few months ago. I wasn't feeling my oats, so to speak, and I thought I was having a stroke. I went to see my good doctor friend, and he suggested I take a good sniff of his medicine. It was, he said, a medicine which was centuries old, an ancient Indian remedy."

"How could he do it all those years? Didn't the drug enforcement agencies get after him?"

"Well, let me go back a few years, after he became really successful. The money was rolling in and his practice grew enormously, and I think almost everyone in the city must have switched to Dr. Tisherman. He relocated in a new big house, joined the country club, bought a home in Florida and a ski chalet in Vermont. The children went to private school, his wife had a new car almost every year, and everything seemed swimmingly well. Then the good doctor started to get bored. It wasn't so obvious at first.

"He began to miss his dinners, and then he'd come home a bit later each night. You guessed it. He had a lady friend, a charming youngish woman—likeable, tall, efficient. The patients liked her, and so did the doctor. She was the model secretary, and beyond that obviously more. The good doctor went to more and more medical meetings. He planned everything in a meticulous manner—or should I say cunning. She became a friend of the family. His wife enjoyed her company, and she did her best to help his wife out with her correspondence or whatever else was needed. When they took trips to Europe, they brought her along so she could act as a babysitter for the children.

"How do you know all these things?" I asked.

"Tisherman told me everything. His lady friend came to talk to me, too. Much of my time is spent listening to other people's indiscretions.

"The young secretary had other boyfriends—younger men than the doctor—truck drivers, bricklayers, roofers—all unknown to Dr. Tisherman, of course. It was really she who started him on all that was to follow. First, she introduced him to marijuana, which he was very reluctant to take, but he did it for her, and, after a while, the marijuana began to please him. Soon, they started on cocaine, and she suggested that he could write prescriptions for it. Dr. Tisherman became less bored and began to change.

"He worked with more energy than before, and took on sports that only a young man would hazzard. He bought a motorcycle, and his blonde friend kept ever urging him on, now complimenting him on how handsome he was, then on his youthfulness and strength. He actually began to look younger. He certainly seemed it."

"One day, I decided I'd better take a look into what was going on. After all, I was his friend, and now he was a dashing figure racing around town on a motorcycle. He came to see me and was sitting where you are sitting now, his eyes glowing like diamonds. His speech was rapid, colorful, non-stop, as if someone had wound him up, as if, as they say, he was wired. I told him, 'You're changing so fast, I can't keep up with you. Do you have any problems you'd like to talk over?'

" 'Me, problems? By God, no! Things have never been better. I love my work, and I'll probably get a bigger office. Why do you ask? Did one of my patients complain about me?'

" 'No, nothing like that, except . . . Well, you know, the motorcycle, the young lady. . . .'

" 'The young lady is my secretary and friend, and my wife cares for her as much as I do. She's like family now. She shops with my wife, she baby-sits for us, and she's a loyal friend and a great secretary, nothing else. Understood?'

" 'And what else?'

"He stood up straight, indignant. His eyes flared at me in anger.

" 'Nothing else! I'm in love with my wife and my children. You have no right to put me on the spot like this.'

"He was so angry that he walked out of the house, and I watched him through the window suddenly begin running straight down to his house, leaving his motorcycle behind.

"I wanted to see more for myself, so that night I went to the high school gym, and there he was, playing ball and running with the teenagers. He wore blue shorts, a white sweat-shirt, and behaved as if he was one of them—sweating and laughing, carrying on with the boys. Towards the last half of the game, he was running and screaming for someone to pass the ball, when he suddenly fell, and lay very still. When I ran over to him, he was clutching his chest and breathing heavi-ly. They brought him to the hospital. A heart attack.

"He survived, and two months later he was back at work, doing twice as much as before, if that was possible. He wouldn't hear about getting a partner. This was all some five years ago. He had his coronary when he was 35, and another complete change took place in him. He shed his mod cloth-ing, groomed his hair carefully, dressed immaculately in dark shades, wore only shoes imported from England. This occurred overnight, it seems. He had become so meticulous that he even developed a compulsion about how his shirts were to be laundered. He found an English lady who would do them by hand. The odor of the soap told him if the shirts had indeed been laundered by this English woman. If they weren't, he flew into a furious rage. He dressed like an elegant physician practicing in the early twentieth century, like one of London's Harley Street consultants in a black jacket and striped pants. Twice a year he took his wife to Harrod's in London and arranged to have a tailor send him his ties and shoes, even his underwear and handkerchiefs.

"He made lots of money and there was no end to his spending. Dinner had to be served on linen tablecloths, in Rosenthal china and Waterford crystal, a butler—dressed formally—doing the serving. He hired a French cook to prepare gourmet dishes. At first, his family found it all a treat, but the children soon couldn't stand the routine of dressing each night, and Dr. Tisherman began to eat alone with his wife. They kept moving into bigger houses until he found a mansion with a winding staircase, surrounded by old oaks and majestic hedges, overlooking Long Island Sound. He developed a carriage practice—a gentleman practitioner—and kept increasing his fees. His poorer patients, of course, had to find other physicians. As his clientele became even wealthier, his eccentricities only increased.

"Each morning, it became a ritual before he left to spend one hour grooming his face and body with all sorts of creams and pomades, inspecting each new-found crease, unhappily following the lines on his face as he would the markings of a road map. Fresh flowers had to be on his desk, as well as in his lapel. His obsession with aging and seeing the older patients arrive with their chronic complaints caused him great despair. He researched the entire problem of aging and the forms of treatment being used primarily in Europe, placental injections, concoctions of gonads, mixtures, procaine, vitamins and cocaine. It was after reading Freud's description of cocaine that he decided that he would use it in his own practice. Cocaine was immediately and impressively effective. His use of it increased. He told me about his plans, but I couldn't dissuade him. He was driven, possessed.

" 'Freud perhaps may have written much of his great theory of psychoanalysis while on cocaine,' he said. 'Great surgeons, like Halsted—who devised the first hernia operations, gallbladder surgery, mastectomies—did their most productive work on cocaine.'

"He was the Halsted, he thought, of the 1980's."

"He tried his first treatment on a patient by the name of Jake Abrams, a lonely miserable soul who was well into his eighties, a man who had lost his wife and son and was the only remaining survivor of his family. Each day, Jake prayed for death to come. His health was reasonably good, but he did suffer from the early stages of senility as well as arthritis of the joints. Jake had plenty of money, so he went to all the clinics and saw the most renowned specialists throughout the country. Tons of pills and treatments were tried on him, none of which helped. Besides being depressed, he lost his appetite and began to lose weight. It was against his religious beliefs to commit suicide, which he would otherwise have eagerly accomplished. Just to pull himself out of bed and dress took half the morning. It wasn't that he was terminally ill, but that he was so full of pain and despair that he wished only to die.

"Each week Jake came to see Dr. Tisherman, who gave him his special treatment. The old man began to change gradually. He smiled more, paid closer attention to his personal care, and, by the end of three weeks, became a dapper gentleman, impecably groomed, carrying a silver cane. It mattered little to him what it cost. For the first time in years, he had the will to live. He refurnished his apartment, got himself a girlfriend, and even went back to his life-long hobby of painting.

"And so it went, more or less, with all the others. Their lives became bearable. Old hopeless women now appeared lively and youthful and optimistic. Word spread like fire in a dry forest, and Dr. Tisherman had to turn patients away. Time on his waiting list stretched to many months. He selected only the most desperate and hopeless. One look into his waiting room and it became quite evident why he was so successful. Happy faces—eager, alert eldery patients—delighted with life. He devised fantastic ideas of actually buying an island in the Caribbean and converting it into a complete Paradise for the aged, Eden reborn for the elderly.

"Then, one week ago, on a particularly hot summer day, three men arrived at his office and served him with a warrant for his arrest. The patients watched, startled and disheartened and disbelieving, as agents escorted him out. He was arraigned and released on bail. A horrendous scandal was about to break. The federal authorities confiscated the hundreds of vials of cocaine that he had in his office. His wife and children, in a state of shock and bewilderment, were staying at their summer home in Easthampton. Dr. Tisherman returned to his own house and changed into a pair of slacks and a wool shirt.

"One of his neighbors saw him take a shovel from the toolshed and march out to his garden and begin to dig a trench. He had taken an extra large dose of cocaine and was digging furiously for hours, until he dug a trench six feet long. He was perspiring freely, but not weakened for one moment.

The cocaine gave him the extra strength that he knew he would need.

"By sunset, he had accomplished what he'd planned. Only now he began to stagger, to become increasingly weaker. He was a good enough physician to recognize that his damaged heart could not have tolerated such strain and heat. The garden's where they found Dr. Tisherman. Dead. Sprawled in the ditch. The newspaper reported his death as a tragic heart attack that occurred while he was working in the garden.

"His wife and children were left with ample insurance money, but, unfortunately, tragically, he left a practice full of addicted patients—that's what he left for you to take over, if you still want to. Can you now understand why I said that Dr. Tisherman is better off dead?

"But I'm troubled by persistent questions. Was it really so wrong, what he did? He was, after all, rendering a medical service to a lost generation of elderly people, burdens to their families, unwanted and misplaced individuals. He gave them new hope and aspirations, reasons to live. He gave them peace and even cheer."

"Unfortunately, Reverend," I answered, "cocaine gives a false temporary euphoria, and it is only time before it destroys the reason, the very soul. There are no shortcuts in caring for the sick and lonely. Cocaine is not the answer. Dr. Tisherman used his patients to justify his own addiction."

Leysin

THE TRAIN RIDE from Lausanne, Switzerland, to Leysin took forty-five minutes, winding through the beautiful valleys of the Swiss Alps. It was the winter of 1952, and I was on this train heading for the famous TB sanatorium. The sanatorium was located on top of one of the magnificent Alpine mountains, and the train stopped at its base. The air here was clear and dry, and the mountain was covered by miles of sparkling white snow. Everything, including the sanatorium, was white, except for the elevator—a freight elevator that carried the dead back down the mountain to the train that would take them back to Lausanne. It looked like the freight elevator in New York that lifted cars to their parking spots.

Fifteen medical students were crowded into this vertical moving bus, which had a medicinal smell. Fifteen medical students ascended to meet TB patients for the first time. We had come to learn about the most dreadful disease of the century.

We took little notice of the beauty that surrounded us because of our fears and anxiety of what lay before us.

Not far from this sanatorium was a renowned health and ski spa where healthy people went to enjoy the pleasures of the grand tranquility of the mountains and the air.

A pleasant-looking nurse met us as we stepped off the elevator and escorted us to the lecture hall. It looked like the rotunda in most other medical schools, except this one was surrounded by glass that gave view to a white paradise of glistening snow and the awesome surrounding mountains. The lecturer who was going to give us the preliminary talk on TB was as tall as a giraffe wearing a long white coat.

"I'm Professor Michaud. I have TB, mostly cured, and I have been in this sanatorium since I was a medical student like you."

His opening remarks left us unnerved because, each year, one or more students contracted TB and was forced into a sanatorium for cure. Antibiotics for the treatment of tuberculosis had not yet been discovered. The only treatment consisted of the "open-air method." Rest and exposure to the sun, along with drastic surgical treatment, such as pumping air into the stomach or chest to collapse the diseased lung. Sometimes, attempts were made to cut the TB cavity free from the lung.

I was assigned two female patients; one was in her late sixties, and the other, Gabrielle, was twenty-three years old.

Outside on a large open terrace, patients in under-clothes were strewn on long folding chairs lying in the sun like skiers resting between slaloms.

A long white corridor was lined by private patients' rooms. Each door had a plaque with the name of its tenant.

My older patient was Madame Corot, whose name was written on a small gold plaque. A pleasant voice answered after I knocked. Sitting by the window was a gray-haired woman, knitting, wearing a colorful shawl around her narrow shoulders. "*Entrez.*Please come in and close the door. We don't want a draft, do we?" she said.

"I am the new medical student assigned to examine you."

"Oh, I know, it is the beginning of the month."

"You speak English very well," I told her.

"Thank you, that is a compliment coming from an American. Actually, I taught myself. I have the time to do it. Please sit down. Would you like a glass of champagne? It is nearly lunch."

"Thank you, but it is too early for me."

"Ah, yes, you Americans live by the clock. There is a time to eat, to drink, to sleep, to work, and perhaps there is a time set to die, but you are too young to understand all that." She pushed herself off the chair and walked over to the far side of the room to the shelf of a large French armoire that was stacked with champagne bottles.

As she was pouring a glass for herself my eyes roamed around the room. It was richly furnished with a dark oak table, an upholstered chair, bookshelves, a small, round, inlaid French table and a small, four-poster canopy bed covered with a red woven blanket brocaded with golden fibers. Everywhere the room was festooned with rich colors. Ottoman brocaded fabrics and silks upholstered the chairs and benches and there were spreads on the floor. On the walls hung calligraphies of embroidered silk designs displayed in vivid colors. I felt I was standing in the room of the Sultan Süleyman from the sixteenth century.

"My family are Turks, Ottomans," she said. "I was born in Istanbul."

Outside of the room was a large balcony with a blue velvet chaise longue covered by a large canvas to protect it from the rain.

"We have to sit outside on the balcony three hours a day, and when the weather permits, the doctor asks us to sleep outside several times a week, but I am getting too old for these outside acrobatics.

"Now, my young American student, take a chair here and I will answer your questions while I drink my champagne."

With pad and pencil in hand I started the routine of taking a medical history.

"How old are you?"

"The last time I counted I was 61. If it weren't for you students, I would have lost count long ago."

"When was the first time you became ill?"

"Thirty-five years ago, before you were born."

"You have had TB for thirty-five years?"

"Perhaps longer. I was married and lived in the Topkapi Palace in Istanbul. When my child was six years old I became ill."

"How long have you been in Leysin?"

"Twenty-five years. The doctors said I was not to leave if I wanted to stay alive." She continued to talk without my asking her questions, and after one hour, and ten pages of scribbled notes, she said, "I am getting tired. Let us continue tomorrow. It is time for lunch. They will serve it in my chambers, and then I will have a nap, and it will be time for you to take the train back to Lausanne."

The students ate lunch in a common cafeteria used for the staff and visitors. Actually, it was a full dinner that included wine, soup, pork chops, mashed potatoes, and a Napoleon and coffee. Each of the students sitting at my table were relating their first encounters with their TB patients. At first I was reluctant to eat any of the food because the TB bacilli pervaded everywhere in this beautiful setting. But as no one else seemed to share my fears, I ate a delicious meal all for one dollar and thirty cents.

After lunch I went to visit the next patient. Her room was located on the other side of the hospital, at the end of a long hall that smelled of oxalic acid disinfectant. This was the home of the very sick patients, some who were waiting to die.

One of the students informed me that the disinfectant had seeped into the hall from one of the rooms where a patient had died. It had been cleaned and made ready for the next tenant. A stretcher passed covered with a white sheet, carrying one of the dead. They were carried down to the basement where an autopsy was performed. Then they were placed in a sealed brown box and taken down the mountain in the elevator to a special compartment train and back to their homes to be buried. The coffin was not opened again because the TB was still alive in the dead patient.

Here, the patients had numbers, not names, on their doors. After knocking on the door there was no response, and I meekly opened it. Inside there was a bed with a young woman lying in it covered with a white sheet. Her eyes were closed, and she had long beautiful brown hair spread out on a large pillow like a fan. As I was about to leave she spoke in a sweet French voice, "Don't go away. I was only resting. I become so tired after lunch. I was outside all day on the deck. I hate being inside when the sun is out. Are you one of the doctors?"

My ability to speak French was improving, but I still carried a very strong accent. "I am one of the students, here to examine you."

The room was stark and depressing. There was nothing in the room except a bed, a night table and a commode with an empty urinal on the floor. A clipboard hung from the wall, keeping a daily record of the patient's temperature. With my other patient, I had felt intimidated by the luxurious surrounding. Madame Corot had been well indoctrinated by the hundreds of medical students who had visited her, but this poor young soul was afraid, shy, and vulnerable. She lay helpless in the bed like a wounded bird, and she appeared so desperately pale I was afraid she was going to die in front of me, something I could not bear to witness. Gently, ever so softly, I moved the bare chair next to her bed. "I am an American medical student. My French is very bad so be patient with me, and don't speak too fast, because then I won't understand you and you will have to repeat everything again."

She laughed. "I can understand you. Don't be afraid of me. You can sit down. I won't make you sick, but if I become tired you will have to come back tomorrow."

She must have seen the apprehension on my face and the pity in my eyes. Finally, I sat on the chair, sniffing the air, which smelled of the disinfectant rising from the floor.

"They just scoured the floor with that disgusting fluid," Gabrielle said. "It is good to rest. I was outside all morning where the air was fresh, so fresh that it made my body tired. I must be very sick," she sadly said. "Everyday I look to be stronger; instead I feel worse. Is that what is supposed to happen?"

"It takes time to get better. You must be patient," I told her in an unconvincing voice.

"How old are you?" I started on the traditional routine of history taking.

"Twenty-three." Her eyes were like two light amethysts, soft, transparent like the faint lines of a Degas painting.

"How long have you been ill?"

"I am not sure. It was so long ago." Her cheeks were pale

except for two jolly red circles. She kept tugging at the sheet to bring it up to her narrow neck, as if to hide the rest of her.

"I became ill on Easter day with a bad cold and it didn't improve. My father took me to the doctor and they X-rayed my chest and here I am. Simple as that. So it must be six months. Time stands still on the mountains; only the light changes." As she spoke her voice was interrupted by a violent cough and then she began to wheeze.

"Are you all right?" I asked.

"I start to cough when I speak too long. I used to love to talk, sometimes too much. When I lived at home with my parents and two younger sisters, they complained that I never stopped chatting. 'You are a chatterbox,' my mother told me."

"Are you a student?" I asked.

"Yes, I dance."

Her face became violaceous red, the color of begonias in bloom. "It must be early afternoon," she said, "because that is when my fever comes to visit me and stays all night until the first light of day. My body then feels like when I was dancing, warm and sweaty, and my heart pounds. I used to be so afraid when it happened, but now it makes me sleepy. I fall into a deep peaceful sleep and dream. Oh, do I dream! I dream I am dancing on top of the mountain in the cool air, and everything smells good, instead of like disinfectant."

The nurse came into the room carrying a tray with a thermometer and jelly. "Well, I am glad to see you getting on so well with Gabrielle. Turn over, my little ballerina, time for your afternoon forecast. Doctor, you can step outside and have a smoke or something."

"Will you come back?" she asked.

"Of course, but I will have to take the five o'clock train."

From outside the door I could hear Gabrielle's gentle

voice. "Can't you warm it up once? Why do you have to stick it in there? You know it will be high. Put it under my armpit. It is just as accurate."

"Gabrielle, the doctor wants a rectal temperature." Five minutes later the nurse was finished; she gave me a sad, knowing look and showed me the clipboard with the temperature record.

"What was it?" Gabrielle asked. "No, wait, let me guess— 104. Right? I can tell because I am becoming drowsy."

"Here, take two aspirins with a little water and you will cool down."

"And I will sweat and you will have to return to change all the sheets. If you didn't bother taking the temperature, Beatrice, I wouldn't need aspirins and you wouldn't have to change me."

"And the professor will send me out to take care of the cows," the nurse said.

"When you are ready to examine her, Doctor, push this bell, and I will assist you."

"Thank you, but I still have to finish the history."

"Oh good," Gabrielle said cheerfully, "then you will have to return tomorrow and I will be all fresh and cleaned." The nurse placed a small glass filled with a purple solution on her night table.

"It is theophylline," the nurse said to me. "You take it, Gabrielle, and don't spill it out in the bathroom. You know it helps your wheezing. Doctor, see to it she drinks it. It opens her bronchial tubes."

"I hate it. What good is it. I drink it and then it only works for a few hours and I wheeze again."

"Gabrielle, would you prefer a suppository?"

"I will drink the purple poison, thank you."

She folded her milk-white slender arms in front of her and said, "Well go ahead, ask me questions."

The nurse left the room, and I placed my notebook on my lap. Before her eyes were cool and youthful-looking; now they were partially closed and wet. Her body was burning up from the fever. She had small narrow eyebrows that curved gently above her drooping eyelids, as if someone had sketched them in.

"Where were you born?"

"In the Valais, in Sion. Have you ever been there?"

"No."

"Then you must visit it before you return to New York."

"How do you know I am from New York?"

"Because I guessed. I know of three cities in America— New York, Chicago, Hollywood."

"Well, you are right, I am from New York. For a minute I thought you could tell from my New York accent. Did you have any childhood diseases?" I continued.

"Yes, scarletina, mumps, chicken pox, and something else that made my cough sound like a horn, not like the kind I have now."

"Whooping cough?"

"That's it."

I glanced at my watch and it was almost five. "I have to go, Gabrielle, because I will miss my train."

"Come tomorrow after breakfast. My room number is 26, so don't get lost. There are many Gabrielles staying at Leysin, and you will have to start right from the beginning, introduce yourself and all that. And they won't be as patient as I."

"I will remember the number. Have a good night's rest."

"Can you open the window a little before you leave so then I can hear your train leave? I love to hear the train; it gives me hope that someday I will be on that train. Here in Leysin we live by sounds and light and smell, because the mountains are always the same. It is the lights that make it different. These mountains are my cell keepers, but the sounds of the train are the sounds of hope."

As I closed her door I felt a sad indescribable pain in my chest. The train back to Lausanne was crowded with medical students, nurses, and doctors who were free for the evening. As anxious as they were to leave for the city, so I yearned to stay with Gabrielle to look after her. What if she wheezed and coughed bitterly at night, and there was no one to hear? Being isolated like a punished child in a miserable dreary room was bad medical care. She only had a bell in her room to ring for help, but that was hundreds of yards away from the nurse's station.

Next to me on the train sat a student from Zurich who was also in his senior year. His speciality was going to be TB and respiratory diseases. "How do you like our Leysin?" he asked in English.

"I find it fascinating and sad."

"We give them excellent care and most of our patients recover. Dr. Jacquet's treatment has been successful for ninety percent of our inpatients. Our sanatorium has the best record in Europe. It is even better than your famous one in Saratoga. What part of the sanatorium are you visiting?"

I told him about my first encounter with Madame Corot and Gabrielle.

"Gabrielle is one of our most serious cases."

"Will she die?"

"She has not responded to Jacquet's treatment as well as we hoped, at least not yet."

I spent the remainder of the evening in the quiet of my

room reading everything I could find on TB. The signs of worsening TB are a persistent fever, continual weight loss, gross spitting up of blood, and the TB lung cavity not shrinking. As I read, the image of Gabrielle's innocent red-cheeked face seemed to fill the page and I could hear her wheezing. Later I had a fretful sleep.

At seven o'clock the next morning I was back on the train to Leysin. I was the only medical student on board, along with the nurses and doctors and other helpers. The chief of the TB service approached me in the hall of the sanatorium.

"Do you Americans always start your day so early? The lectures will not begin until nine. Come and have some coffee with me."

"I need an earlier start because I haven't really finished my work from yesterday."

"Well, that is noble of you. Our Swiss students know they have all the time in the world. Some wait for years before they present themselves for the final doctorate examination. This is our system. I know in America there is no such laxity."

It was the end of November and the mountain air was damp. The clouds hung over the mountains like white curtains.

Ward B was deserted except for two orderlies pushing a stretcher with a body covered by a white sheet. I stopped short and wanted to pick up the sheet. Instead I rushed to Room 26 and found the door slightly ajar. With my hand I slowly pushed the door open, and with great joy and relief, I saw Gabrielle sitting up in bed reading a book of poems by Verlaine.

"Bon jour," I rejoiced.

"Aren't you a little early?" she said.

"I like to get an early start."

Her face was pale, and her eyes today looked like blue

transparent glass.

"How do you feel?" I asked, as I still was standing by the door waiting to be asked inside.

"My fever came as usual, but it didn't stay so long. I feel much better, stronger, but you can't examine me until I am cleaned up and the sheets are changed. Come back at ten. But it is nice to see you so early. I expected you on the second train."

She looked remarkably better to me. "I guess Dr. Jacquet's treatment is beginning to work," she said with a smile.

"Then a little later I will return," and I closed the door behind me and bumped into the morning nurse who said sarcastically, "You might as well have stayed over."

My face became crimson as I scurried away from Ward B to see Madame Corot. Two women carrying the same illness; the older one in stable condition, and then Gabrielle, desperately ill. That was the instructor's intent—to demonstrate the range of TB in 1952.

Madame Corot was in her chair where I had left her the day before. "Good morning Doctor," she said. "You are an early riser. That is good; it shows a strong character and devotion. I, too, have been up early. I have already taken my morning walk. A half-hour walk followed by a glass of fresh orange juice and then yogurt with fruit, ementhal with bread, and three vitamin pills. Last night I slept on my balcony for two hours in the cold air, which was invigorating, youthful. Did you ever read Boccaccio, Doctor, *The Nightingale*? You should. Then you could understand how I felt last night outside."

"Does Dr. Jacquet include champagne in his treatment program?" I asked in all seriousness.

"No, but he believes if the mind is well then cure is

inevitable, and if a glass or two of champagne makes patients happy, he allows it. The professor believes the TB bacilli does not like good champagne, but the brain does. Do you know his theory, why people catch TB?"

"I don't," I said. "He has not lectured to us yet. Actually, I never met him."

"Oh, you will. If you don't meet him I will introduce you. He is a remarkable man. Not only is he a great doctor, but he is a major in the Swiss army. Now, to his theory: he believes people who have had terrible disappointments and who suffer from melancholy will develop TB or other diseases.

"My illness started when I was a young woman living at the palace where I worked as a private secretary to the sultan. My husband took up with the governess of one of the royalties and ran away with her, leaving me with a six-year-old child. I became so depressed that I planned to kill myself. At the palace they tried all sorts of potions and hydrobath cures. They soaked me in ice water and then put me into a steaming bath. The doctor of the palace was convinced that I had to be isolated from the palace. They placed me in a cell-like room, on a water diet with vitamins. I began to lose weight and still was dreadfully depressed. As I was all alone with no man in the prime of my youth, the wise man concluded it was necessary for me to have an operation to remove the excitable part of my body, the circumcision, as they called it. They removed my clitoris in one quick swipe of the razor while they administered ether."

"Where was this done?" I asked in a state of disbelief.

"At the palace there was a women's clinic for deliveries and other operations."

I remember reading that this type of barbaric treatment of women still existed even in 1950 in the Sudan, Kenya, and parts of West Africa. Circumcision of women was prescribed by Mohammedan law. Even in modern Egypt this operation was still performed on peasant girls.

"But this, too, did not cure my depression. And when I began to lose more weight and develop night sweats and started to cough blood, they diagnosed me as having tuberculosis and then sent me here to Leysin twenty-five years ago. You see, my young friend of twenty or so, the TB bacilli likes to live inside of unhappy people," she continued. "But you will learn about all of this while you are here. Even in so many of our famous stories, the heroine dies of TB from a lost love, like *Manon*. I became ill because of my misfortunes."

I wasn't convinced then or to this day that an illness could be caused or cured by the state of the mind alone. It is cured by a brilliant, marvelous drug that kills the bacilli. Antibiotics for TB, when they were discovered, closed all the sanatoriums in a few years as they cured the patients. So it was with every illness we have had, and today, AIDS and cancer will have to be cured with the magic bullet, once it is found, and not just by thinking good thoughts.

The nurse arrived one hour later and Madame Corot was undressed and put into a hospital gown. I examined her lungs, heart, and stomach, and when I was finished I had found no abnormalities.

"Well Doctor—what then should I call a second-year medical student?—you found nothing. I am glad; it means I am getting better."

I thanked her for allowing me to examine her and then proceeded to the lecture hall where Jacquet was to give his talk. As on the first morning, he never arrived, instead his assistant described the terminal aspect of TB.

The X-ray department was located on the ground floor

and was attended by a Russian doctor called Boris Babiantz. I found Madame Corot's chest X rays, and then hand-carried them to the reading room where Professor Babiantz was sipping coffee and smoking a cigarette.

"We haven't taken a film from Madame Corot in years," he said. "She refuses to be X-rayed. This one was taken five years ago," he said.

We both looked at her films—he with his expert eye and I as a novice. "Are you sure these are her films?" he asked.

"This is what they gave me."

"According to these films, she no longer has active TB," he said. "In essence, she is cured. We perform X rays on the patients once every six months. There must be other films on file."

We looked through the old files in the basement and did locate her chest films from ten years earlier, which demonstrated the classical TB signs, a large hole, or a cavity, in the lung.

"How does she feel?" the radiologist asked.

"She complains of fatigue, but I did not find anything on the examination."

"Well then, ask the doctor in charge of her case to order some sputum collections. The TB bacilli is found in the sputum, and in some cases even in the urine. According to the number of TB in the sputum, the TB is classified as to its infectability as 1+ to 4+. The latter indicates a marked contagious stage, and then extra precautions are taken by the staff."

At this sanatorium there seemed to be no signs of anyone taking precautions, such as wearing masks and gloves when examining the patients. At the beginning of each stay at Leysin the students had a skin test for TB and a fluoroscopic examination of their lungs, which was then repeated again before they left. Most of the doctors who stayed at Leysin developed a positive test for TB. A positive test meant that a mild form of TB had been contracted.

As I was leaving the X-ray department to return to see Madame Corot, I met Dr. Jacquet. His bald head looked like a shiny bowling ball set with two large dark eyes that looked like onyx stones. He was a small man, but with large powerful arms and legs. And when he shook hands with me I could hear my fingers crack from his solid grip.

"I hope you will enjoy your stay here in Leysin," he said slowly in English. "My office is open to you if you have any questions or problems." With that he disappeared, like Peter Rabbit scurrying into the hall. I never saw him again for the rest of my stay in Leysin.

It was eleven o'clock in the morning when I returned to visit with Madame Corot. The sun still had not broken through the clouds and the mountains were not visible. There was the dampness in the air before it begins to snow. She was sitting on her chaise longue on the balcony, wearing sunglasses even though there was no sun.

"The lights up here are so strong," she said, "that they hurt my eyes." She was wearing a Persian lamb fur coat and a Persian hat, looking like a Russian princess riding on a sled.

"I am sorry to bother you again."

"This is no bother," she answered. "What else is there for me to do?"

"I want to ask you some more questions before I write up your report."

"I know about the report, how important it is for the students. You are very serious. Relax a little, young man. You will be all worn out before you are thirty. You must save some of your energies for the better things in life, if you know what I mean. Well, go on then, ask some more questions."

In the European medical school system there were no examinations until the end of the year, and most of the learning was left up to the student, except for the medical reports that, it was rumored, the professors never read.

I asked Madame Corot again the same questions.

"As I told you Doctor, I am only tired, and if I do just what the doctor tells me, I get by each day. It is almost lunch. Can I offer you a glass of Moët? I have had enough of the balcony for now, and I must write some correspondence before lunch because the mail leaves at three."

I was glad the interview was over because it was raw outside, and I felt my bones shake from the cold air. Or was it from her dark Turkish eyes piercing me?

Dr. Duvalle was the immediate doctor in charge of Madame Corot. He was a man about fifty years old with gray hair growing out of his nose. He had an expression on his face as if he were always smelling something foul. His lips were curled up towards his nose. We barely exchanged greetings, and when I asked about collecting sputum from Madame Corot, he gave me an annoyed look and said, "When you write your report, include that as part of the suggestions," he said.

"But would it not be better if I had the sputum results so I can write a thorough report, including the prognosis?"

"Your 'stage' will be finished in a week or so, and it takes several months for the culture. Unless, of course, you would like to stay here for the rest of the semester and wait for the cultures to return in two months?

"Oh, by the way, it is not necessary for you to arrive here at seven in the morning unless you want to help in the kitchen to prepare breakfast."

He was an obnoxious doctor, and I would be meeting

many more like him in the future. How can such an insensitive man work with patients? I wondered. But when one of the patients strolled past him, he was remarkably charming and warm. He transformed into a different person—the doctor was not the same person as the man who had told me to become kitchen help.

After lunch I was on the large terrace, which looked like a deck of a luxury ocean liner. Although there was no sun, and the sky was covered with great ominous clouds, the patients were lying on chaise longues, barely dressed, taking their outdoor cure. I was shivering from the damp air, but the patients tolerated the cold better than I.

Gabrielle was lying on one of those chairs, covered with a light sheet, still reading her book of poetry. For a few minutes I watched her from a distance. Her long brown hair came down to her shoulders, and her face had a peaceful look. She was the youngest one on the terrace today. Occasionally, she looked up, giving a pleasant greeting to a passerby.

"Hello, Gabrielle. Aren't you cold?"

"A little, but I get used to it. Dr. Jacquet said it is the best thing for me. I missed you this morning. I was all cleaned up, waiting for you to examine me."

"I know. I am sorry. I had to see another patient."

"Was she pretty?"

"Yes, but not as pretty as you. She is old enough to be your grandmother," I said.

"Pull a chair over and sit a little while with me. Then we can go in, and you can examine me. You are wearing a different tie today," she said.

I had not noticed it. I just grabbed any tie because I rushed out to the train.

"You are as old as I am, I bet," she said.

"Just about; perhaps a year or two older."

"Do you have a girlfriend in America?"

"No."

"How about here in Lausanne?"

"No, Gabrielle. I have no girlfriends. I am too busy to find a girlfriend."

"You are a cute-looking guy. I bet there are plenty of girls who would like to go out with an American medical student."

"Well, I have not met them yet."

"Do you like to dance?"

"No, I don't know how to very well."

"I could teach you when I get better. I would like to dance for you."

"I would be honored, Gabrielle."

"It will take me a long time to get back into shape. Ballet is really hard work." She moved her small body under the sheet as if she were standing by an exercise bar in front of a mirror.

"I dance *Petrouchka* the best, and *Swan Lake*. Have you ever seen a ballet?"

"Yes, I saw *Swan Lake* in New York, and the *Nutcracker Suite*."

"I was invited to the Metropolitan Ballet School for one year, but then I became ill," she said softly. Her eyes became moist, and I felt a sick feeling in the pit of my stomach.

"Can you take me back to my cell," she said. "I am getting chilled. I think the fever is coming back."

I wheeled her back to the room under the suspicious eyes of the other patients.

"Now, if the other doctors were as thoughtful," teased the nurse from the morning, whose name was Nurse Marais, "it would make our work easier."

"Can you help me? I have to examine Gabrielle for my write-up."

"It is not necessary," Gabrielle said.

"It is a hospital rule, Gabrielle. No doctor examines a female patient without a nurse, especially young, handsome, male medical students."

The nurse gave me a knowing glance. Nurse Marais had that mature look of an understanding woman. She was a large woman who reminded me of the actress Simone Signoret. It was obvious she cared a great deal about the gentle Gabrielle, not only as a patient but as if she were her daughter.

I waited outside the door as Gabrielle was undressed and made ready for the examination. "Come on in, doctor of the future," I heard Nurse Marais yell. "I just took her temperature for you, Doctor, and it is normal for the first time in weeks. You bring good luck to Gabrielle."

I looked into her mouth first and found her tonsils to be small, but not infected. I examined her tiny ears with an oto-scope, and I could hear her breathing close to my ear. Nurse Marais undid her hospital gown and held it in front of her chest as I proceeded to examine her lungs. I tapped the back of her chest to find areas of dullness and areas that would sound like a drum if there were a cavity underneath my hand. I could not find any of these abnormalities until Gabrielle said, "You have to go higher. That is where my cavity lies. Here," she said, and twisted her hand in back, touching my hand.

She was right. The tapping sound changed dramatically to a sound like a drummer playing. With my hand flat on her chest, I asked her to whisper "33," which would give me a clue if the lungs were filled with fluid or contained a cavity. My stethoscope on her chest moved slowly each inch as I heard both lungs wheeze and rattle and gurgle like a sulfur geyser I had once heard on a volcanic mountain. I moved to the front of her chest and Nurse Marais dropped the sheet, revealing her youthful body. Gabrielle's face flushed, and she closed her eyes as I listened to her heart.

Before the invention of the stethoscope in the 1800s, doctors placed their ears directly on the patient's chest. Besides causing all sorts of embarrassing problems for the female patients and doctors, there was also the fear of catching fleas from the patient, which was what prompted the great youthful clinician Laennec of France to remedy the situation by the invention of the stethoscope. All of Europe made a mockery of Laennec's "tube" for almost fifty years. The American Supreme Court Justice Oliver Wendell Holmes even wrote a humorous poem about Laennec's stethoscope.

In Leysin the older doctors, on occasion, still placed their ear directly on the chest for better hearing of the sounds of the heart and lungs.

The front of her chest was wheezing as loud as the back, and her heart was racing. Her eyes opened, and she looked directly at me as I listened to her heart under her breast. I felt my face turn beet red and swiftly moved away as Nurse Marais re-covered her moist chest.

She started to wheeze more than ever, and Nurse Marais poured some theophylline into a glass which Gabrielle swiftly drank. "Do you make all your patients wheeze?" the nurse joked.

"Only if they are allergic to me," I quickly replied.

"Very clever, doctor."

Gabrielle was now lying on the pillow. Her face had

turned a purple-red, but her wheezing had subsided to some degree.

"I am very sick am I not . . ." she said with a sad, desperate voice.

"Not so sick, Gabrielle. I have seen others who are much sicker and get better and cured."

"You better learn to lie so it doesn't show on your face, because no patient will believe what you say."

"Look, Gabrielle, I am only a medical student. You are my second case of TB. I have examined you and you ask me questions like I was some kind of expert. I really don't know how sick you are."

"Don't get annoyed. I was only trying to get information."

"I am not annoyed, just frustrated."

"Well, then you need a girlfriend."

Nurse Mantis gleamed with pleasure as we carried on this way. She reminded me that the last train was leaving in minutes.

"Are you coming early again, before the rest of the students?" Gabrielle asked.

"Of course I am. I have to look at your X ray and write up your report and that of the other patient I examined. Well, have a good evening."

"I will miss you until tomorrow."

I wanted to tell her I would miss her too, but I dared not.

Nurse Marais accompanied me down the long hall and said, "You did very well. She is very sick, the poor sweetheart, and she cares a lot for you."

"And I for her," I said.

"When is your stage over?"

"In a few days," I told her.

"Don't tell her unless she asks. She has no friends here

and does not get many visitors, except once a month her parents come. She is so young and beautiful," the nurse continued, "and she is a dreamer. She resents the doctors and all the people who can come and go freely. I am always afraid she will do something foolish."

"Like what?" I asked in panic.

"Like leaving her bed at night and walking to the edge of the terrace and throwing herself down the mountain."

"But that can't be possible. She has to be watched then all the time."

"That is not possible."

"Has it happened?"

"Yes, but they are usually older ones who take the stroll to the bottom."

Back in the city that night I wrote up the case of Madame Corot while I kept thinking about Gabrielle. It was a long ten-page report, and my conclusion was that Madame Corot no longer had active TB and could be discharged from the sanatorium at any time.

The following morning I chose a bright red tie and blue shirt and took extra time to comb my hair. I brought a bouquet of white flowers for Gabrielle. The sky was cold and gray when I arrived at the top of the mountain. This morning the hospital looked deserted. Then I realized it was Saturday and most of the students and staff would be off until Monday morning.

Gabrielle was sleeping peacefully and her face looked angelic with some beads of perspiration on her white forehead. Sleep is a blessing for the sick; it is the only refuge they have from the horror of the reality of their illness.

Dr. Duvalle, the obnoxious doctor of the floor, greeted me coldly as I arrived on Ward B. "I finished my report on Madame

Corot," I told him.

"That is very good. Leave it on my desk and I will grade it and return it to you on Monday. What is your conclusion?" he asked.

"I think she no longer has active TB."

"You are likely correct. Why don't you tell her the good news. She will be most grateful to you, and then she can leave, and Dr. Jacquet can chalk up another cure."

Madame Corot was sitting at her table in the center of the room. The table was covered with a gold brocaded Ottoman rug, and she was sipping coffee from a small cup.

"Will you have some real Turkish coffee?" she asked. "On Saturday, I treat myself with this luxury. You are an enthusiastic young man. Have you come to examine me again?"

"Well, I came to tell you some great news about your illness."

"I always like to hear good news. What is it?"

"I spoke to the doctor, Duvalle."

"He is not my doctor. My personal doctor is Dr. Jacquet. Anyway, go on."

"You no longer have TB, and you can leave the sanatorium."

"Are you sure?"

"Well, I think so. Dr. Duvalle agrees. I wanted to tell you the first thing in the morning. I was so excited."

She remained silent and quietly sipped her coffee. "Where is your report now?" she asked. "I would like to see it."

"It is in Dr. Duvalle's office."

She slowly moved up from her chair, faced the icon on her night table, and placed her hands together as if to pray. "You fool," she started quietly and then began to scream. "This is my home. I can't leave here. Where will I go? I have no home like you. I have been here for twenty-five years, and you tell me I am cured. How dare you say that. Dr. Jacquet knows I am still sick. I can't go out there. Please leave this room and never return. I can't leave here until I die!" she screamed and began to sob like I had never heard a person cry so desperately before.

Dr. Duvalle had heard the screaming from the room and was at the door when I left.

"What happened in there?" he asked. He saw my pale face and smirked with delight.

"I told her she was cured. Why didn't you tell me I shouldn't?"

"You didn't ask."

"You knew all this time she did not have to be here?"

"Yes. We sort of let her stay here and go along with her madness, but now it will have to change."

"Why?"

"Because she will have to come to our weekly conference on whom can be discharged. You will be back in Lausanne completing your studies and get a wonderful recommendation for your thorough work, and she will be out on the street."

"That is insane. Why blame it on me? You assigned me to the case."

"Unless of course, you want to withdraw your report, and you will get an incomplete."

"I am not going to hold back on the truth," I yelled at him.

"That is your choice, sir."

This was my first lesson on the mystique of the practice of medicine. As I have learned over and over again, some people will never forgive you for trying to help or even save their lives. Madame Corot was using her illness to keep a roof over her head. I later learned that her stay in Leysin would be paid for as long as she remained. It was her choice to make this her life home. Actually, the doctors were being humanitarians by going along with her madness. Or had they been doing her a great disservice by not having forced her back to the mainstream of life years ago?

The radiologist on call for the weekend was well acquainted with Gabrielle's illness. He swiftly retrieved her X-ray films, and in the darkness of the room he uttered a sad sigh.

"If you look here, she has two large TB cavities which are not healing. That corresponds to your physical findings," the doctor said. "We collapsed the lung once, called a pneumothorax, which did nothing to help her. Medical treatment is a continual game of hits and misses; luckily most patients get better despite their treatment."

He saw the forlorn look on my face in the darkness of the X-ray room. He offered me a cigarette. "It doesn't look good for her."

"So you think she will die?"

"I am not a medical doctor, just a radiologist. My life is lived in the shadows of the day and I deal in shadows. That is the question you have to address to Dr. Jacquet when he returns. Some patients live on for months, others for weeks, and then there is always the chance a cure for TB will be developed. They are not too far from it now. There is a doctor by the name of Waxman, in Boston, who has been working on such a drug.

"You have a special interest in this case?" he asked me.

"I care a lot for Gabrielle. She is too young to die."

"We all do. She is as gentle as an edelweiss flower on our mountains. Her sputum is swarming with active TB bacilli," the radiologist continued. "She also has a heart murmur that has developed since she's been in the hospital."

"A heart murmur? I did not hear one. I examined her just yesterday."

"It is not easy to hear. One of our interns picked it up and the cardiologist confirmed it. That is another one of her problems we have to solve. She doesn't have rheumatic fever, which is so common today in our young people, and the heart murmur is getting louder."

This was not a good day for me. First I caused great chaos in Madame Corot's life, and now I had completely missed a heart murmur. In my write-up of Gabrielle's case, I would have flunked miserably if I had failed to find the murmur.

"Go and listen to her heart again and you will hear it. That is why you go to medical school, to learn. Don't look so downcast. This won't be the first time you will miss a heart murmur. Why do you think I became a radiologist?" he laughed. He placed his arm about my shoulder and again said, "You can only become a doctor if you care and if you experience failure. It makes you humble and more careful. It is not the end of the world."

Gabrielle was sitting up in a chair by the window, her hair now tied in a ponytail with a small red ribbon. "Thank you for the paper narcissus. They are beautiful."

"How are you feeling?"

"Better, but a little sad. Look outside." The entire world outside was painted white. The mountains were no longer visible and the last few red autumn leaves were now off the trees. It was snowing heavily, like in the heart of winter.

"Snow comes early to Leysin and never leaves," she said. "Professor Jacquet makes us lie out on the snow when the sun is out with only our underclothing on."

"Gabrielle, I have to listen to your heart again."

"How nice. You know it makes me a little nervous, but

only when you examine me. I love your beside manners. You are so gentle."

"I am going to call the nurse. I will be right back."

"You don't have to call the nurse. I trust you."

"I'd rather call the nurse, Gabrielle."

Nurse Marais, luckily, was working the weekend. She was sitting at her desk, busy writing in the charts.

"I am sorry to bother you, but could you help me again? I have to listen to Gabrielle's heart."

"You did already, yesterday."

"I know, but I missed a heart murmur completely. I can't write the report up until I hear it."

"It is Saturday. All the students are gone. Why don't you go back to Lausanne? Come back on Monday. I am the only nurse on for two wings." She looked at me again. "When you get that puppy look on your face," she said, "you and that little ballerina, I can't resist. All right, come on. You have ten minutes."

"I need five."

This time I listened to Gabrielle's heart first while she was sitting up and then lying down, and the murmur was there. It came from one of the valves of the heart, but I was not certain from which one.

"Why are you listening so much? Do I have heart trouble now? If I do, it is all your fault."

"Thank you, Nurse Marais," I said.

"Will you be back today?" Gabrielle asked.

"Yes, but I have to write up your case before I forget everything."

There was a large comfortable library with easy chairs, tables, and good lighting. I described my findings in detail and wrote my conclusions, which troubled me because my only diagnosis was pulmonary TB; I still was left without an explanation for the cause of the heart murmur.

It was past five P.M. when I finally finished the long write-up, and it was dark outside. The snow fell furiously with wind howling circles around the sanatorium.

When I returned to Gabrielle's room the nurse told me the trains would not be running until the morning because of the storm.

"Oh, wonderful. Then you will have to stay here all night. Thank you, storm," Gabrielle said.

"I suppose you will want to eat here with the princess," the nurse said.

With not much resolution I said, "I will eat in the cafeteria."

"I will bring you a tray, too, and perhaps through some sniffing around I can find a carafe of wine. You worked hard today and you deserve it. But don't go shouting this to the other students because then there will be trouble."

One half hour later, Nurse Marais brought two trays, a small white tablecloth, and two candles with a carafe of red wine.

"There now, my *petite, bon appetit.*" She returned minutes later with a blanket and a pillow. "In case you decide to sleep on the chair next to mademoiselle."

There was a small radio in the room and Edith Piaf was singing, *"Mon Homme,"* my man.

"Do you like the Little Bird too?" Gabrielle asked.

"She is my favorite singer," I replied.

I lit the two small candles on the round tale and ate the usually unappetizing hospital meal, which tonight was like a feast. The candlelight's glow made Gabrielle's face appear languid and beautiful. We ate the small pieces of ripened Camembert while sipping on the wine for dessert. Gabrielle's face turned red. At first I thought it was the wine, but it was her night temperature rising. She tried to suppress a cough, and then her wheezing became audible in the room. She rose from the table and opened the drab-looking blinds.

"I have to open the window just a bit. It helps me breathe better."

Snowflakes settled on her brown hair as they sped through the window. She took a swallow of the purple medicine by her bedside and the wheezing began to subside. From her dresser she brought out some photographs of herself and placed them on the table like a fortune teller.

"Perhaps it will be the worst snowstorm of the century, and you will have to stay here for days with me. Would you like that?"

"Yes, I would like that very much."

"These are my parents in front of our house, and my two sisters."

"They all look like you," I remarked, "not as pretty."

"Do you think I am pretty?"

"Of course, very."

"Much prettier than any of your girlfriends?"

"Yes, if I had any girlfriends."

"Then you really like me?"

"Yes, of course I do. I like you a lot, Gabrielle."

She gave me a sweet coy smile and loosened the little ribbon which held her hair. It came falling down her back as gently as the snowflakes were foiling outside.

"This is me dancing." She produced a photograph of herself doing a pirouette, wearing her leotards. Other photographs followed, showing Gabrielle in her *Petrushka* costume. She looked at the photographs with an anguished expression on her face.

"I will never dance again," she said in a solemn voice. "You saw my X rays, did you not?"

"Yes."

"Well, they must be pretty bad. When do you think I will die?"

"That is ridiculous! You don't know what you are saying. If you are going to talk like that I am going to leave."

She started to cry. I wanted to cry with her. I sat next to her and placed my arms around her small soft shoulders.

"You did that to get my sympathy Gabrielle, and it won't work. You will be cured in a few months and you won't even remember me when you get back to your stage life."

"Then I will be all right. Are you sure? I believe you for tonight. Because tonight is a magical night. I feel so alive for the first time since I came to Leysin. God sent the snow to keep you here for me. I want to dance for you."

"I want to see you dance, which will be very soon."

"Not very soon. Now. tonight. I feel strong enough. You step outside and I will put on my leotards. Return in a few minutes. Dr. Jacquet said that some exercise is good for me."

"Gabrielle, you can't dance now. You are not strong enough. You might harm yourself." She started to undo her robe. "All right. All right. Call when you are ready."

When I returned she was dressed in her leotards, and she looked adorable. Her hair was now drawn into a bun, and she stood bent over slightly with her delicate arms crossed over her side. Slowly she moved her body gracefully, with her arms stretched, circling in mid-air, and then she was on her toes circling the room, then jumping in the air as I stood entranced by this strange scene. For a moment we were both transported to a recital hall. Beads of perspiration appeared on her forehead as she bounced from one end of the small room to the other. Her eyes always focused on me. Then she stopped, bowed her head and knelt down as I applauded.

"That was beautiful, Gabrielle. You are incredible."

"Did you really like me?"

"Yes, I'm speechless."

She fell back on the bed, wiping her forehead with a towel.

"Now I am tired. I want to take a little rest, but you now have to read to me with your cute French accent from my poetry book. Here," she said, "read *The Living Flame* by Baudelaire. I will close my eyes and imagine we are in a small café in Paris on the left bank, and we are sipping on fine cognac and coffee and it is late at night."

I started to read the beautiful poem out loud. One of the lines I was fearful to recite: "They sing of Death, you sing the Resurrection;... Bright stars whose brilliance no sun can dull!"

Gabrielle was sleeping soundly and I covered her perspiring body with a blanket. I sat in the hard, uncomfortable chair, scrutinizing her labored breathing. This was the first of many more times to come when I would be sitting by the bedside of a critically ill patient. Sweet Gabrielle, so young and innocent. Why should she be suffering so much? I could not imagine the world without Gabrielle.

Several hours later she awoke, uttering a soft gentle sigh, as if she were returning from a beautiful dream. I was sitting in the chair finishing up her case history.

"You are still here while I am sleeping. I am sorry. You must be so bored."

"Actually not, I was doing my homework."

"Writing about me? I hope it is nice things." She pulled the vase of flowers from her night table and held them close to her bosom.

"These are so beautiful. No one ever gave me flowers like this. Now I know you like me a little."

She sat up and her face blushed. "I never had a man, and I am going to die, no matter what you say. Do you like me a lot?"

"Yes, you know I do."

"Do you think I am sexy? You did see me when you examined me."

"I remember well."

"Well?"

"Well what? You are a beautiful young woman."

"Do you like my body?"

"Gabby, that is not a question to ask."

"You called me Gabby. No one ever called me that."

"In America, you would be called Gabby."

"Will you do one thing for me tonight, because tonight is my night? It was given to us."

I feared what was coming next.

"Make love to me. You don't have to kiss me, just touch me. I just want to know how it feels. I dreamed you did. It was such a heavenly dream. No one would know, and I would not betray you. You don't have to kiss me, because my mouth is filled with the deadly bacteria, and I wouldn't want you to get sick. You are too sweet and dear to me."

I wanted to race to her and place my arms around her to protect her from the angel of death, but she saw the anguish on my face and began to cry, "I am sorry." She cried herself to sleep while I sat motionless and confused on the chair, not knowing what to do.

When early morning finally arrived, I silently crept out of the room as she remained in her peaceful sleep. The trains were running again. Outside it was still dark. It stopped snowing and a sliver of moonlight reflected on the white night. The snow was as pure as the young woman I had left. I did not need a Hippocratic oath to convince me how I had to behave at that enticing moment, and my vulnerability would be many times tested during my medical career. Falling in love with a patient is one thing, but to take advantage of a woman who confides all her trust in a doctor is despicable. I wanted to maintain the doctor-patient relationship with Gabrielle and act as her healer rather than her lover, lest she lose all respect for me.

I watched the sun rise over the Alps from the train, which moved slowly through the snow-packed tracks. When I arrived back at my small room in the hotel where I was staying, I had decided that I was going to care for Gabrielle. This was the first time I had ever felt so deeply about someone. I would speak to the chief of the service to get permission to see her every weekend until she was well, not as a student but as her friend.

I spent Sunday in the library and then searched for a present I would give her on Monday morning. All the stores were closed except a tobacconist, and I found a funny-looking cowboy made of marzipan.

On Monday morning I took the five o'clock train to Leysin. My heart was pounding with anticipation of seeing my ballet dancer. I waited for the freight elevator, which finally arrived. There was a body in the elevator on a stretcher pushed by two orderlies. The Monday morning transferring of the dead. When I arrived at Ward B there was no one on the floor. The hall smelled of oxalic acid disinfectant. Gabrielle's door was opened and inside a woman was kneeling on the floor with a pail, scrubbing the walls. The bed was empty.

I raced outside, looking for the nurse or doctor. There was an older man and a woman standing by the nurses's desk. I recognized them from the pictures that Gabrielle had shown me. They were her parents signing some papers, and they were given a bag of clothing.

"Where is Gabrielle? What happened?"

"Gabrielle is in heaven," the woman said and started to cry.

"She died on Sunday," Nurse Marais softly said. "She died in her sleep."

I looked at her parents and felt I had known them all my life. Her mother had the same face as Gabrielle.

"Did you know my daughter?" the father asked.

"Yes, we were friends for a short time."

I had to look away because tears filled my eyes.

In the following weeks, streptomycin was introduced for the treatment of TB in Boston—the miracle drug that arrived too late to save Gabrielle. I never returned to Leysin again. In spite of my medical report, which I had submitted, Madame Corot was permitted to stay until the sanatorium closed, for the new treatment of TB had cured most of the patients.

Many weeks later I found the picture of Gabrielle in her leotards on the inside of my jacket pocket. She must have slipped it into my pocket while I fell asleep at her bedside. It had a small inscription written, "This is how I want you to remember me," and she quoted one other line of the poem we had read together: "You sing the Resurrection of my soul."

Bel Air Mountain Lodge

THERE WAS ONCE a very special hotel in the Catskills that served as a haven from the hot summers of New York for a group of greenhorns, as we were called then.

Hitler was marching through Europe, and we few, we lucky few, had escaped the massive slaughter which was about to begin. My father anticipated what the murdering Germans were planning and devised a precise plan of escape years in advance of what was to come . . . but that is another story.

Lucia, my mother, was an adorable petite woman, a social butterfly, a hopeless optimist, with cheeks as scarlet as ripe tomatoes, and a charming, irresistible smile. It was her brain-storm to start this very special hotel.

"You can't breathe in the city, I don't want to spend another hot summer sitting on those uncomfortable park benches all night down on Riverside Drive, just so we can get some air." My father and her many friends spent those horrid hot nights on the Riverside Drive park benches, waiting for the breeze to rise from the Hudson River, singing German and Polish songs and exchanging stories, until early hours in the morning. My older brother and I slept on the fire escapes or on the roof of our apartment building on West End Avenue and 99th Street. Sometimes we got lucky and we spotted a young woman undressing in front of an open window, and we forgot about the airless night.

"What do I know of hotels," my father said, when mother suggested a small inn in the mountains. Two years earlier he was a rich, renowned industrialist coal dealer in Danzig and mother was the grand lady of our large estate surrounded by servants.

We escaped from Danzig to America with only the clothes we were wearing and money sewn into our underwear.

Lucia made friends easily with the Americans in spite of her fractured English. In a few minutes of conversation she knew all about them: if they were married, what their business was, and how much money they were earning.

One of Lucia's new American friends was a man who ran a lingerie store on 48th Street and Broadway. He was a tall, tough-looking Irishman, with fiery red hair, green eyes, and a fat large nose like a hippopotamus. She bought her slips and underclothing from him because they were cheaper than at the neighborhood stores and with her coquettish ways was able to reach his soft side. It turned out he owned a large abandoned guest house in a small village, Napanach, located in the Catskills.

The year was 1940 and America was still in the tail end of a long depression. "Greenhorns are going to ruin this country, that is why things are so bad here, they take away all our jobs, become rich."

"Mr. Jim, we are not rich, I don't work, and my husband is

trying to sell coal," mother told him. That is the reason he did not put my mother into this derogatory category.

The inn stood vacant which my mother swiftly found out, with a few innocent questions. "It must be beautiful up there high in mountains," she said slyly. "Is it expensive to stay there?" "The place is empty, and has been empty for a year," he answered with an annoyed, gruff voice. "What a shame, empty so long," she said as the wheels in her brain were churning for a plan. She invited him to dinner although she had not cooked a single meal in her entire thirty-five years of life. Father did the cooking and my brother and I washed the dishes. She made him laugh by her coy way of using the wrong word in a sentence. "I will bake a cake for you and get some West to make it big." "You mean yeast don't you?" the Irishmen asked. "East, West what's the difference. It will be a good cake." She bought a pot roast and got instructions from the butcher about how to cook it. "We will give him lots of whisky and beer to make him happy and the dinner will taste good. And then we will ask him if we can see his farm," she said. "It is not a farm," father said, "it is an inn. This is a crazy idea, I know how to run a coal company, shipping, barges, I don't know the first thing about a hotel." My father had shipped coal and lumber from the port of Danzig to England and the continent, and he knew nothing of the hotel business, except where the best hotels where located in Europe.

It turned out this Irishman did not drink and he cooked the pot roast himself in the small kitchen of our tiny two-bedroom apartment which was infested with roaches and mice.

My brother and I used the same kitchen to cook our breakfasts which we ate there.

It was also the place where the dumbwaiter bell rang each morning and we had to drop the small breakfast table from its hinges, open the dumbwaiter door, and pull on the rope that lifts the platform to our apartment. Then we placed our garbage on the platform. This acrobatic maneuver, which we performed every morning, gave the roaches a chance to invade the four-by-four kitchen from the reeking open elevator shaft. The kitchen work table was replaced as well as the breakfast dishes, and my brother and I alternated making fried eggs and bacon, our quotidian breakfast.

The following week, on a very cold Sunday morning, the Irishman, whose name was Jim O'Brien, agreed to drive all of us to his Inn at Highmount, located at the base of Bel Air Mountain. It was the heart of winter and it was miserably cold. His old wooden-paneled Ford station wagon had no heater. I wore my ear muffs and shivered for three hours as we drove up on the old 9W highway. I did not hear much of the adults' conversation but they did a lot of laughing and moving their hands.

The hotel was a large white clapboard house, with a long veranda, standing on top of a hill surrounded by a spacious lawn covered with a thin sheet of ice making it look like a large frozen pond. On the dirty front door window in large black letters was a sign that read, "Christians Only."

"No wonder he has no guests," father told my mother in German. "He is a Nazi, and you want this place?" Jim did not notice that father's face twisted with anger. Jim was as accustomed to the sign on his door as the shutters on the windows—it was a part of the house. Jim pushed opened a weather-beaten door. "We don't lock doors around here, there are no other houses within a thousand yards, and all neighbors are nice decent people, no ruffians or foreigners." We walked into the entrance hall and breathed in the smell of a pine forest.

At first sight we loved the old house because it was quaint inside with beautiful pine wood walls and floors; it was nicely furnished with clean-looking couches, chairs, small round tables with hurricane lamps, and an enormous fireplace with photographs of sailing ships sitting on a dark oak mantle.

From each window, through the naked trees, we could see a spacious frozen lake and, rising above an entire valley of cottages, the majestic Bel Air mountain. Tall pine trees with tear-drop icicles hanging from their branches encircled the house. A winding staircase led to four bedrooms and another narrow staircase to a large airless attic furnished with four small bedrooms. It reminded me of the story of Goldilocks and the Three Bears. The small entrance hall led right into the living room, and there was a large dinning room to the right of the hallway containing seven round wooden tables covered with stained table cloths. In back of the house, there were five little white bungalows with blue shutters sitting in the pine forest. The whole scene looked like a Currier & Ives Christmas card.

Mother convinced Jim to rent the house and the bungalows to us for the summer season. For security, she offered him a diamond brooch she used to wear just a few years ago whenever she and my father attended the opera.

"Lucia, you are impossible. How could you do that? He will run and sell the brooch for five times the worth of that shack we just rented and retire to Ireland and drink himself to death," my father told her in German on the way back to New York in the car. Father was a practical man, a once very successful business man who was now working for Blue Coal as a salesman and was an independent distributor of Polish films. He earned a meager wage that was just enough to get by in those depressed times.

"He will not, Henry—you don't trust anyone," Lucia said. "He is a nice man, and he does not drink." Although Lucia did seem a bit uneasy because she had spotted a strange little grin on Jim O'Brien's weathered face.

With the help of her refugee friends, Lucia rented a small apartment on West End Avenue to organize a club for the newly-arrived refugees from Europe. It was called the Club for Greenhorns. They met to talk, and prepare for the citizenship examination and drink tea. Most of members were former lawyers, doctors, judges, artists, actors, industrialists, business-men and women who had escaped from Hitler, and were now working in factories and restaurants, even doing street clean-ing for the city of New York.

During one these meetings of The Club, mother announced "Ladies and Gentlemen, this summer you are all invited to our country club home, with gourmet food, with a lake for swimming and boating, and tennis courts, at a rea-sonable weekly price, to escape hot New York." Everyone cheered and applauded, and she added, "Opening of Bel Air Hotel begins this Memorial Day week-end. Make your reser-vations now to be certain there is room for you, with a deposit of ten dollars."

Every Sunday morning my father, my brother, and I stood freezing in front of the Catholic Polish church handling out leaflets announcing the exciting Polish film to be shown that afternoon. I dreaded those mornings and I was in terror when the priest appeared at the entrance of the church. He was a very tall man with large shoulders and scary eyes. I was afraid he would learn we were Jewish and would drag me into his church and do harm to me just as the tough boys from

Amsterdam Avenue and Holy Name Church who attacked us whenever they got a chance, screaming and beating us up and blaming us that the Jews killed Jesus Christ. We could never walk home from junior high school or go to Riverside Park alone because these hooligans were there waiting to attack us. Father gave me little choice and I had to go those Sunday mornings by subway to Brooklyn, and to make things worse, Lucia gave us leaflets to hand out at the church announcing the exciting new hotel FOR CHRISTIANS ONLY AND NO DOGS. The Polish priest was so pleased that his parishioners would have an inexpensive place in the summer that he gave a blessing for the new hotel "where Christians can meet together during the summer months." My parents had a big fight about that announcement since all the guests of the club were Jewish.

Many members of the club swiftly sent their deposits as most of them were my parents' friends. By March more than one hundred and fifty people had made reservations but the hotel had room for only seventy five. Fifty of the reservations were made by the priest of St. Maria church in Brooklyn where we distributed the leaflets. We were all very pleased since now we had enough money to renovate the old house, and we had enough money to open the hotel on Memorial Day weekend.

"Where will you put all those guests, we hardly have room for fifty people," father said in German to Lucia as we sat around our table in my brother's and my bedroom which served as the dinning room and the study. When father was very serious he spoke to mother in German, when he was in a sweeter mood he spoke to her in Polish. I had no trouble understanding either language. "If worst comes to worst, we will refund the people from Brooklyn and send a note 'Jews only,' " she laughed.

"And they will deport us to Cuba," father said. "We are not citizens yet, don't forget that, Roosevelt just turned back of boat load of Jews who escaped from Europe."

When Spring arrived we went to our little hotel in the center of the rich pine forest to begin the clean up. Father painted the rooms and my brother and I washed the windows, polished the furniture, tables and chairs, and cleaned all dishes, pots and pans, and silverware. Mother prepared the menus and arranged the housing and seating arrangements. It was a much bigger job than we anticipated. The work went slowly but by the beginning of May the hotel began to take shape.

Lucia sat at one of those wonderful roll up desks in the living room on a high stool that made her feel tall and important. She wore glasses that were bent out of shape and tried to decide where guests would be seated for dinner and what rooms they were to occupy. These foreigners where no ordinary people. Each of them had a respectable and even prominent position in Europe but now were reduced to subaltern menial jobs. Seating them at the right table with the right people was a herculean job.

"My friend, Junio, where will she sit and sleep? She is the only single woman and so beautiful. We can't have her with Anspach, the banker, because his wife is so jealous. I know, I forget Leon Pommers is coming. The pianist—they will get along fine." She mumbled to herself for hours placing people in little circles on a dining room plan she constructed.

I was appointed the bus boy and my brother was the waiter. My job was also to care for an old upright coal stove in the basement used for heating water for the main house. And I took charge of five weather-beaten wooden row boats, attached to a decrepit-looking dock leaning like the Tower of Pisa on the crystal clear spacious lake. A long, narrow path overgrown with prickly bushes descended from the hotel through the woods to the lake. Another one of my more difficult and tedious chores was to cut the bushes, clear the path and paint the boats with three different colors: red, white, and blue. That was mother's idea—an act of patriotism. We had to wait two years more before we would receive our naturalization papers. After suffering the heinous acts of the Germans, becoming American was a cherished dream of ours.

Father hired a pretty young Polish woman to be the chambermaid. I became smitten with her, just at the time my male hormones took charge of my body and mind. My brother, who was four years older than I, was going to be drafted in the army in a few months and was busy with his own love affair. Lila, the chambermaid, did not have same turbulent effect on him as she had on me. She only spoke Polish but she loved to work and was grateful to be in the country away from the city, and so was I.

Everything was organized for the opening of the hotel but we did not have a cook. Lucia interviewed a number of candidates but she found none that suited her. They did not know how to make rolled cabbage with meat, or Schnitzel ala Holstein, Flanken, or a soufflé.

She went to visit Jim O'Brien in his Broadway lingerie store to ask his advice.

"I used to be a cook on a merchant ship for fifty men," Jim said. "And I cooked special dinners for the officers," he told her. "Let me be your cook. I will close the store for the summer; things are slow anyway. I'll organize your kitchen and cook whatever you wish. I can learn how to make Jew food, and Polish and German, and you can make me a partner, so to speak. Just give me a percentage of the profit. No salary. I will bring my own knives and things I still have somewhere from my ship days." "That will be wonderful," mother said, "I will give you the menu, and you know how to fix things too?" "Lady, I can build a house, do the plumbing, electrical wiring, anything," Jim said in a loud, proud voice. Lucia was excited to have Jim with us.

On the weekend before Memorial Day Jim cooked us a superb meal, starting with a grapefruit, of roast beef, mashed potatoes, and lemon carrots, and ending with a delicious chocolate cake for desert. He worked alone in the kitchen and we were delighted with his culinary skills. Lucia was happy to have an Irishman in the kitchen who was "so tall and strong and could protect us from the Jew haters."

The week before the grand opening father worked furiously in the house and I helped him shellacking the floors. I was able to get an excuse from school a week before Memorial Day because of "family hardships."

At the end of each day father and I went to a local diner and ate hamburgers or lamb chops and listened to songs by Nat King Cole or Margaret Whitting on the juke box. Sometimes we just sat in father's old wooden station wagon and listened to the "fights" on the small radio. Joe Louis was fighting Jack Dempsey that night and we rooted for Joe Louis to win since he beat Schmelling, the German, in his last fight. Father loved Lux Radio Theater and I was enthralled with *The Green Hornet* and *The Shadow*. The news from Europe was disastrous. We heard how the Germans invaded Poland and concentration camps were established. I spoke to father and mother in English after I was humiliated each day in school, being called a greenhorn because I did not know the language. It was then I decided to learn to speak like an American, lose my accent and never speak German or Polish again. In the years that followed not one of my classmates learned I was born in Europe. "Do you think Uncle Herman and all our aunts and grandmother and grandfather are alright?" I asked my father one day after the Joe Louis fight. "I don't know," father said. "On the Polish radio program I heard the Germans took all the Jews into the camps." "What about Astor," I asked. Astor was my German shepherd that I loved and we had to leave him in the house with my German governess when we escaped. We told the authorities we were going to our summer home in Sopot by the Baltic sea. We left our beautiful home and I kissed Astor good by. He knew we where leaving. He lay back on his bed with his head and eyes looking so forlorn. The captain of father's trawler took us to Southampton and there we caught the Queen Mary to come to America. "The Germans like dogs," father said. "They are right now in Danzig and taking good care of him." I saw the sadness in my father's eyes and I knew he was lying just to make me feel better. "We are very lucky that we could leave," father said in a subdued tone. It was years later that I learned the real story of our escape. He had planned it for years in advance of the war but the triggering event occurred because he accidentally killed a German while driving his car and he was to be arrested the next day, the day we left. Because he was such a prominent man as a major coal distributor to various countries including Germany, the police captain (father's tennis partner) treated him with respect and secretly told him to leave immediately. From him, a year later, we learned the Germans were living in our large home in Danzig and our entire family had been deported to the concentration camp where they eventually perished.

That was probably the only time I felt close to my father during that one week as we sat in that old car and chewed on Tootsie Rolls, and Mars Bars and drank cream soda, and laughed a lot. "If the Germans did not come," he told me, "I was going to teach you and your brother to horseback ride, ski, play tennis, and when you got older you would never have to worry about money, because we had plenty, and you could if you wanted to come into the business or do anything you wanted, go to medical school or law, anything." For the first time he related to me how wealthy we once were and told me more about his successful business. In Danzig he was too busy with his business and social life, always traveling with mother throughout Europe, leaving me with the young pretty governesses who raised me. Now in America he was fighting to survive.

Mother stayed in the city and took care of the business part of hotel.

When Memorial Day weekend arrived, mother reluctantly returned the deposits to the fifty people from Brooklyn with a letter of regret that we were all booked up.

On that Thursday it started raining and it was cold and damp. It felt more like March than May. The dining room tables were decorated with miniature American flags and small red roses. Lila, the chambermaid, had each bed made, and I followed her around like a puppy dog offering her help in the bungalow. Sometimes I had the feeling she sensed my carnal desire because more than once she gave me a maternal kiss on my cheek after I helped her make a guest's bed.

On Friday morning it was still raining; and by the evening when the guests were to arrive it rained harder. All of us, including our Irish cook, stood on the porch waiting for the cars to arrive. Mother looked a perfect hostess. Dressed in a long black gown and high heels, she looked elegant and beautiful. Lila the chambermaid was dressed in her provocative tight black inform with a tiny white cap on her auburn hair. My brother and I stood next to her wearing white shirts and black bow ties—monkey suits, as Jim called them.

By one o'clock in the morning fifteen guests had arrived. We expected fifty. No more came because it never stopped raining.

Mother kept our spirits up fluttering from table to table like a dragon fly, checking to see if everyone had enough to eat. As so much food was left over, my brother, with Jim's blessing, offered second servings as I whisked around clearing dishes. Dinner was over at two-thirty in the morning. Father looked pale and worn out, but mother, a night person, felt exhilarated—for her, it was just one big party and the guests had a most agreeable time. As for me, I was too tired to be disappointed with the poor turnout and weakly sauntered through the torrential rain back to the four-bedroom bungalow used for the help. Mother and father slept in the main house, in the attic rooms. The sexy Polish maid next door to me was fast asleep. I often peeked through her window to catch a glimpse of her but my timing was always off—she was in either in bed already, or dressed to leave.

Saturday did not bring any more guests and we all crowded in the living room because outside a gale was blowing. Inside there was a cacophony of laughter mixed with Polish and German chatter. No one seem to mind that the weather was so terrible because they were all having a good time. I built a blazing fire in the old fireplace and luckily my father had enough sense to open the draught in the nick of time. As the afternoon moved on the room was filled with the delicious odors of roasting meat and baking bread, mingled with the sweet smell of burning pine wood. Jim was preparing a special meal for us, and father was helping him in the kitchen to make fruit desert with ice cream. Junio, the only single woman, a delightful young person in her late thirties, one of mother's close friends, was playing Canasta with Leon Pommers, a pianist, flirting in French with him as they were playing cards oblivious to anyone else in the room. She later whispered to Lucia and they both giggled like school girls. Other guests were reading, playing bridge, and discussing the war in Europe. One of the guests, Sol Berney, a former professor of literature and philosophy in Berlin, was sitting in front of a chess board. He looked like a scarecrow to me. His scant gray hair was uncombed; he had a narrow pale face with hanging pale eyelids and a hanging jaw. His physique was lean and unathletic. Sol Berney wanted to practice his English and asked me to play chess with him. It turned out he was a grand master and gave me chess instructions and when I began to yawn he switched to playing Russian checkers. Whenever he spoke, it was in a slow deliberate tone, carefully worded and always with a word of advice. He said things like never lie, a lie always comes out one day; read, the more you read, the better you will understand your surroundings; like in chess, he said plan your next move ahead of each day, and be prepared for the worst if you want to survive; don't daydream too much. I wondered how he detected some of my flaws because I did have a tendency to daydream and occasionally slip into a make believe world of my own—an erotic world with Lila the maid. I did daydream a lot about Danzig and my dog Astor who used to escort me to the school at night to protect me from the nefarious brown shirts who lingered around the streets like a pack of wild wolves looking and waiting for Jewish children by the trolley car I would board to school.

Before the Germans officially marched into Danzig they had a strong presence along with the Hitler youth, who were all good German boys. One of the first ordinances was not to allow Jewish children to attend school during the day. Many times, they threw stones and bricks at my governess and me, but Astor would chase them away. (Perhaps my Uncle Herman sent Astor to America and he would come running up the porch stairs.) My governess, who had taught me how to read and write in Gothic German, was strict on manners. I had to click my heels, bow my head and proffer my hand, whenever I greeted anyone. I swiftly broke the habit after my first day at school when the students laughed hysterically at me. Sol Berney's words rang true. His wife was a huge grotesque-looking women who sat alone quietly knitting like Madame Defarge. I had just finished *A Tale of Two Cities* and I pictured her to be a Polish Madame Defarge.

Late Monday afternoon, as the guests departed, it stopped raining and the sun arrogantly appeared. We lost a lot of money to say the least. Our Irish cook, with a disheartened voice said, "You people aren't so bad as they say, you are pretty nice people, and your bad luck will change. I will give you an advance on my share, so you can try again for the big weekend."

"We have the fourth of July," Lucia said, "and the whole summer, don't worry we will get it back, and let's give Jim a bigger share of the profits," she told father in German. "Like giving him a share of the air," he answered. "Don't be so pessimistic, you will see," she told him in her usual upbeat way.

The fourth of July week-end was a success, as mother predicted, and the summer was on its way with lots of scheduled guests to come to the hotel. Mother and father moved to the little bungalow where the help roomed, because they rented their more expensive room in the main house. Although we were expecting it to happen at any day after the fourth of July weekend the news that my brother had been drafted into the army came as a terrible blow. Mother lost her usual happy glow and cried hysterically as we took my brother to the bus station. Father was quiet and reserved but his sadness was written on his face. He served in the Polish cavalry during the Polish Russian war in 1917, and he knew what horrors might lay ahead for my brother. I became depressed but I felt proud of him and wished I could go too. "You will have to be the waiter and busboy," my brother told me as the wrought iron gate closed and just before he boarded the military bus. Father hired an older man named Eric, a Swede, who became the waiter, because the job waiting on tables would have been too much for me. I remained the busboy and was put in charge of the coal stove water heater in the basement and the waterfront with its three wooden boats. Three times a day I had to shovel coal into the stove, which provided me a chance to be alone, to think and day dream. Adjacent to the stove was an orange crate that served as my place to sit and watch the embers from the coal light up the room. Sometimes, I fed the stove with pine wood and a sweet odor came forth. In town my brother and I had bought pipes and Mixture 79 tobacco which I had hidden in my coal sanctuary. Mixture 79 gave off a pleasant smell as I puffed on my pipe with no fear of being caught smoking by mother or father. One day, Jim came marching down the cellar while I was sitting puffing away. I quickly dropped the pipe, and it rolled on the floor to his feet. He looked at me in the room lit from the glow of stove and shook his head, "I just came down to check," he said. "You shouldn't smoke, it could stunt your growth." I was terrified he would tell father but I never heard a word more said about it.

In the evenings the guests sat outside on small ice cream parlor chairs in a big circle singing songs in Polish and German and telling stories of bygone days in Europe. I sat on the grass against a tree, transported to another time as I listened to these stories of Marinbaden, Paris, and the cafes in Vienna and Warsaw and the rich lives they had led. I could only recall the horror of the German boys in their brown shirts and leather short pants attacking me on the streets each day when I went to school.

In the middle of the summer there arrived a lively young group of guests from Lake Placid. They told off-color jokes which I did not understand, laughed all the time, and sang nightly a song which in later years I understood: "Roll me over in the clover, roll me over and do it again."

The youngest and sweetest of this ebullient group was a pale, secretive-looking fourteen-year-old girl called Ann, she had blond dusty hair, milky blue eyes, and skin as white and soft as down, sprinkled with tiny brown freckles. Mother did not have to urge me to entertain her as I was obliged to with some of the guests by playing tennis, ping pong, or taking them rowing on the lake. Ann had a reticent way about her. She walked as straight as a proud princess; she ate her food the European way, fork in her delicate left hand, pointing downward, not stabbing her food, and the knife in the other. She spoke softly and was well mannered. And when she smiled her perfect line of white teeth shone brightly, but her eyes were always sad and reticent. Her family, friends of mother, stayed in the city. Her older sister fell into the company of some young rich American college students who went to Lake Placid and took her along. Mother invited Ann to stay at the hotel for a few weeks after her sister left.

Ann and I took long walks far from the hotel. I held her
hand, and we talked about the books we read, and our
changed lives in the new world. One day after I finished the
lunch clean-up I asked Jim for some lemons and made lemonade. Then Ann and I went into the pine forest and spread out
a blanket. I kissed her for the first time. She told me she was
taking ballet lessons at the Metropolitan Ballet School and that
her goal was to become a ballet dancer. "But I think I am too
old already," she told me. "I have to learn to twist my thighs, and
it is so painful these lessons, because my teacher said I should
have started when I was five or six years old." She wore a
friendship ring and removed it from her finger, opened it and
gave the other half to me. "Now" she said, "that binds us as
long as you wear that ring." After that first sweet kiss we held
each other and kissed whenever we were alone. I wanted to
touch her beautiful bosom but was afraid she might become
angry with me. Each day I waited anxiously to see Ann in the
morning as she came into the dining room for breakfast and
she would give me a slight knowing smile, and I would dance
around her table removing her grapefruit and rush to clear
the other tables and down to the furnace room to check the
stove. We would meet by the lake where she would be sitting
in one of the wooden rowboats reading, wearing her blue
two-piece bathing suit. I would swiftly jump into the boat to
row far into the lake before any of the guests would come. On
the far side of the lake was a large smooth boulder. It looked
like a little stone island. "It is a small fragment of a meteorite
that fell into the water just for us," I told Ann. It was our little
island where Ann and I docked our rowboat. Spread-eagled in
the sunlight in our bathing suits we held hands and kissed
and watched the clouds moving and the birds soaring above
us and sometimes we watched fish jumping. Then when our

bodies became too hot we dove into the cool crystal lake to cool off, which was a necessity for me. All the guests seemed to take little notice of Ann and me except Jim, who gave us suspicious glances whenever we disappeared and I arrived late to set the tables. He never became angry except once when I took all the lemons from the vegetable bin to make lemonade. In the evenings we found another little hideaway in an old barn that father said we would one day turn into a recreation hall for dancing. We took some candles, and a blanket from my bed and placed it on the straw floor and Ann read poetry by E. E. Cummings to me. She never said much to me but always had a little smile on her pale, languid face. We made plans to meet in New York: I would meet her at the Metropolitan Ballet School after her dance lessons and we would have coffee and walk in Central Park, and be lovers forever. The two weeks passed so quickly and when I took her to the bus station down the road from the hotel she kissed me and promised to write me every day. After she left I busied myself playing tennis and ping pong with guests and sitting by the stove in the dark smoking my pipe and thinking of Ann. She never wrote or answered my letters and would not speak to me on the phone. I wanted to run away from the hotel and go to New York to visit her—perhaps she was ill and could not write. I was too embarrassed to ask mother what had happened to my sweet Ann. Not a minute passed in the day when I did not think of her. At once I became angry and depressed that she was ignoring me. It was a game for her, a brief summer romance, but for me it was crushing. I took the ring off my finger and threw it in the lake as I stood on the once-magical boulder where we had sat and kissed. I never returned to that rock again and the lake looked ugly to me from then on.

As the summer passed into late August, we had new guests: an older married Italian couple that Lucia lassoed into coming to the hotel at a reduced rate. They had just arrived from Italy taking a circuitous route through Cuba. They spoke French, Italian, and a few words of English. Lucia said they were Italian nobility. The woman's name was Mellisa and her husband was called Alfredo.

He was tall and thin, with a head of black hair and deep serious eyes. His wife was as tall as he, had short brown hair and skin as white and languid-looking as Ann's. She always wore a long dress, high heels, and a smart hat to shield her from the sun. It was uncanny how she resembled an older Ann. I wondered if they might be related, but Ann was from Germany and they were Italians. If I closed my eyes it could be Ann's soft sensual voice speaking each time I heard Mellisa speak Italian or French. Alfredo wore a leather hunting jacket flung loosely over his shoulders. With his knickers and black weathered boots it made him appear even taller. I suspected that was the only clothing they owned because they wore the same outfits for the entire week. They both looked like they had stepped out of a story book, or from a Italian movie. They smiled politely, but they did not talk to anyone. Alfredo always took Lucia's hand and kissed it when he arrived for breakfast. Mellisa only spoke to Lucia, her only friend in America. Alfredo and Mellisa looked like they were glued together. Her arm was always locked under his and they walked together tall and proud with their heads up as if they were being filmed, strolling in their summer garden in Venice. They both had jobs working in a diner on 8th Avenue and 43rd Street in New York and lived in one room on Tenth Avenue. Lucia learned that Mellisa was an opera singer at La Fenise in Venice and Alfredo's family were part owners of a Murano glass factory. They had to escape because they openly opposed Mussolini and were going to be arrested and sent to the newly-organized concentration camp. They left their luxurious estate located on the Grand Canal and arrived penniless in America. Lucia met Mellisa at night school in the local junior high school where English lessons were being taught for the new arrivals to America. For two years Lucia liked going to the night school because the teacher was young and friendly and she liked meeting the new greenhorns. When Mellisa came for the first time to the class they swiftly became friends. America is a miracle, she told my father, the aristocrats are brought together with the bourgeois; both once rich, they would have not associated with one another, especially a Jew and a Christian. Now they shared being poor in a new land and class distinction was no longer at play. She spoke French to Mellisa and drank tea at Rupplemyer cafe at the St. Moritz Hotel which was a favorite hangout for many of the new arrivals from Europe. Lucia told her the many times she had visited Venice and stayed at the Grand Hotel by the canal, and she remembered the little palace by the canal where Mellisa and her husband lived. "I probably heard you sing Tosca at La Fenise and we would have never met in Europe. Life is strange *n'est-ce-pas?*" she told Mellisa.

One splendid full moonlit night, the week when Mellisa and Alfred arrived, the guests were at their ritual gathering sitting on small ice cream parlor chairs, and I leaning against a tall oak tree listening to the tales of recent bygone days of Vienna, Berlin, Paris and Danzig. The faces of the guests were bathed in the glow of pale moonlight, the air was soft and romantic and my thoughts became immersed in Ann. How could Ann one day be so amorous and the next day not even acknowledge I exist? The thought tormented me. Alfredo suddenly approached me and said "Don't look so *triste*." "You are too young to be so sad," Mellisa's mellifluous voice added. She spoke to me directly for the first time. "The lake," Alfredo said pointing, and raised his hands and arms from his side, moving them to and fro as if rowing a boat.

"Please," he said, "take us to the lake. To the boat." In the darkness lit by the moonlight, I escorted them along the narrow path that led down to the lake. Mellissa wore her high heels and I wondered if she would stumble and fall. The moonlight covered the lake and cast a mysterious silver glow over us. I pulled one of the rowboats close to the dock and they both climbed into the back of the boat, instead of the front facing me.

They sat quietly, squeezed together on the small seat. I picked up the oars and began to row. They sighed with pleasure as they slipped into their far-away world. Alfredo whispered "gondola," and the moon seemed to shine brighter than before. The bow of the boat seemed to reach up to the sky like a gondola because of the weight of the two lovers. I rowed to the center of the lake where the moon shone brightest and the stars sparkled like little ornament lights. This was the second full moon of the month, Venus and Jupiter straddled the blue moon, as showers of August meteorites streaked across the sky, as if chasing each other. We sat quietly in the moonlight listening to the gentle sounds of the water lapping the side of the boat. I was afraid to turn my head to look at them, lest I break the magical spell that also consumed my brain. I had seen pictures of gondolas in my geography school book that showed a man with black hair and large eyes, with a red scarf around his neck, standing in the back of the boat crooning to the riders. I was almost tempted to stand up in the back of the boat, and use of the oar's pole to the steer the boat.

The silence of the night was broken as Mellisa began to sing softly in Italian. I wished Ann were sitting with me in this moonlight and I were holding her hand with my arms around her soft body and kissing her on the lips. Perhaps if I had done that when Ann was here, she would not be ignoring me now.

We must have stayed on the lake for hours, or so it seemed. And then the bright round moon was covered by some fast-moving clouds. Alfredo tapped me gently on my shoulder and as I turned around I saw Mellisa's beautiful face in the moonlight streaked with tears. Alfredo pointed to the shore and waved his hand to return, but I did not want this enchanted night to end; however, I reluctantly rowed back to the dock. When we arrived, Alfredo gracefully helped his wife out of the boat and then bowed to me and said, "*Grazie* for the gondola." He stared at me and I wondered if he surmised the reason for my lugubrious state. I saw in his dark eyes that he wanted to tell me something more. Something I should know for the future about being in love.

The following morning after breakfast some of the guests took their usual long walk on the country road, while the roaming dogs barked around them as they broke out in familiar Polish and German songs. Alfredo and Mellisa followed behind in silence, arm in arm. I decided to follow Mellisa and Alfredo as my morning chores were completed. I wished that Alfredo or better Mellisa would speak to me so I could ask them if they could explain why Ann one moment was so loving and in the next ignored me.

It was depressingly gray, hot, and humid. A blanket of fog covered the lake. But the singing and gay chatter from the guests softened it like a gentle rain falling on us.

Leon Pommers, the leader of crowd, who would become

violinist Nathan Milstein's accompanist, took a right turn on to a dirt road. "Let us be adventurous," he yelled out in Polish, "let's see where this road will take us now, we have taken so many roads in our life."

"Oh shut up, Leon, none of your ghastly orations!" someone shouted. The dirt road became more difficult to navigate, as it was broken up by small trenches and covered sporadically with horse manure.

"Where is that scoundrel taking us," Junia, Lucia's friend, laughed.

" Manure is good luck. So be sure to step on it," someone else yelled. No one did except me. I stepped gingerly into a small turd pile. Perhaps my luck would change and a letter from Ann would be waiting for me. Mellisa turned her pale face towards me and saw how I stepped into the manure and gave me a slight surrpetious smile which caused me to blush with embarrassment.

We came to a large cornfield surrounded by a barbed-wire fence.

"Look at all that corn," Leon Pommers hollered. "Children, the corn is ripe and we will have fresh corn tonight." He approached the fence, which was several feet higher in height than Leon. "Give me a boost, someone, I will fetch the corn," he yelled. "Hey, Alfredo, you are the tallest, give me a boost." Mellisa gestured to Alfredo not to help.

" It is not right to do that," she whispered.

A damp fog began to spread over the field, and the sky darkened. "We better forget the corn, Junia said, "it will rain any minute, I don't want to get my hair wet."

"So it will rain, but we will have corn. Water from the heavens is good for the corn," Leon answered. "But not for my hair," Junia retorted. Junia had beautiful coiffured hair the color of the ripe corn. She was a small-sized jovial woman, a close friend of Lucia, who at one time was an actress in musical comedies in Danzig. Her previous lovers were mostly musicians, and now she was attached to Leon Pommers, another musician. She married the director of the Danzig Comedy Play House who was thirty years older than she. They went to Trindidad, and she immigrated to New York after he suddenly died of a heart attack in Tobago. Her elderly parents refused to leave Danzig as so many others had done.

"Our bus boy, boat man hot water supplier, tennis, ping pong player and, and—lover, come here and I will boost you across the fence and you can also be the procurer of the corn, your new title," Leon said. And I had thought my love madness over Ann had passed unnoticed. That all sounded like good sport to me. But if my girlfriend left me was I still considered a lover? I felt arms pushing me up in the air and, as I was about to be swung over the fence like a puppet, the cornfield suddenly became swamped with men. Their heads were all shaved and they wore gray striped uniforms, with numbers written on their shirts. They were chained to each other at their feet. Silently, they limped along escorted by brutal-looking men in blue uniforms carrying rifles and smoking cigarettes.

Swiftly, I was dropped back to the ground to where we were standing.

"They are prisoners," Junia whispered. "It is a concentration camp," someone else whispered.

It was an awesome sight to see so many men, old and young, walking like that in this beautiful cornfield. Soon a large brown truck arrived with more guards carrying rifles. They jumped out of the truck and ran, their rifles pointing at prisoners.

"You people, out there behind the fence, just move on," one of guards yelled. But not one of us moved. Why were we standing still when the guards had clearly told us to leave? I did not share the fearful curiosity of the others. I just wanted to run, but I saw Mellisa and Alfredo standing, not moving, watching as if they were part of the scene.

We watched as they unchained the prisoners and ordered them to form a circle. The guards then surrounded them, raised their rifles and pointed at the men. Mellisa raised her hand in front of her mouth staring at the guards, while Alfredo straightened his body, as if he were the one in front of a firing squad. We withdrew from the fence and remained silent as we watched the scene unfold.

Now the prisoners were divided into groups of three. I breathed a sigh of relief as the prisoners were assigned to the different parts of the field to pick the new-grown corn. We had anticipated a slaughter, as the Germans back home had taught us to fear.

Suddenly, I saw a young man not much older than my brother break away from his work group and disappear into the tall ripe corn field.

"Get the bastard," yelled the guard sitting on the front fender of a nearby truck.

"Get out of here all of you," he yelled at us once more, but now with a louder and sterner voice that filled me with terror.

The guards turned swiftly around and lined themselves up as a firing squad, pointed their rifles into the corn field and fired several rounds. There was a loud, sickening moan. After the gunfire smoke cleared, the smell of the gun powder still lingered in our nostrils. One of the guards walked towards a narrow path of ripened corn and dragged the body of the dead young man out by his shirt leaving the dirt path covered with blood. The other prisoners stood silently as the head guard yelled, "Go on with your work. Anyone else want to try to make a run for it?" "My god," Leon Pommers whispered. "That is how it would be." Junia held on tightly to Leon's arm, her face now pale and aghast. The guards with angry voices told us to leave the area immediately as it was government property and they would arrest us all if we did not comply.

I felt the eyes of the prisoners on me as we turned to leave. We almost ran from that field of death, stumbling on the unkempt road, tripping over each other in our efforts to rush back to the safety of the main road and the hotel. Alfredo and Mellisa looked ashen, as if they were sleep walking. They did not run, but walked slowly and deliberately behind supporting each other like two wounded soldiers leaving the battlefield.

For the rest of the weekend, a sadness fell over the hotel. The singing stopped and the guests sat around in small groups speaking in subdued tones of their families and friends left behind in Europe. Most of the news came from rumors and the Polish radio station in New York. We learned from one person who escaped from the Warsaw Ghetto that my grandparents had died of a typhus epidemic. My uncle Herman had escaped and was on the run, and the remains of our large family, dozens of uncles, aunts and cousins, were taken from Danzig and Warsaw to concentration camps. He also told us that German officers were living in our magnificent home in Danzig. I reflected on how we stood paralyzed by the barbwire fence watching the killing. What could we have done?

That night the moon sailed across my window and I could not sleep. I kept seeing the prisoners, and the face of the young man all bloodied in the field. As I stared out the window, I saw the shadow of two figures moving silently in the moonlight. But I was to afraid to make a move. Perhaps some prisoners had escaped and found refuge in our hotel just like us.

The following morning, a Sunday, breakfast was served and the usual raucous conversations were subdued. Father knew of the penitentiary which was located on the other side of the mountain and the prisoners who were hired by the local farmers to work on their fields.

Mellisa and Alfredo did not come to breakfast. Lila said their beds had not been slept in. Father searched throughout the hotel but found no trace of them. "They must have been so upset from seeing the prisoners they just went back to New York," father told the guests.

Swiftly, I left the dinning room and rushed down towards the lake. Perhaps they took a boat out on the lake. It must have been Alfredo and Mellisa I had seen in the shadows of the night before.

At the dock, one of the rowboats was missing. The lake sparkled like diamonds and looked larger during the day than at night. The sun now occupied the center of the lake, where once the moon blinded my senses. I saw a boat in the middle of the lake, just drifting back and forth, turning in circles like a slow-motion carousel. Swiftly, I jumped into one of the rowboats, picked up the oars, and rowed as fast as I could towards the circling boat expecting to find Alfredo and Mellisa. I approached, grabbed the rope of the boat, and attached it to mine. I stood up and peered inside, then climbed into the boat. The boat was empty except for a silk scarf that Mellisa wore and Afredo's leather waistcoat. Inside one of the pockets of the waistcoat, was thirty-five dollars and a note written in Italian.

The police searched the lake and found the bodies of the two lovers at the bottom. That night after dinner Father read the translated note to our guests. "We do not wish to live any longer. We do not deserve to be saved while others like us perished."

The American Foreign Legion

WE WERE A small group of American outcasts, unwanted by our American medical schools, who lived in the Hotel Henri in Toulouse, France.

The year was 1952. I graduated from CCNY and was labeled a radical and a Communist, because I had participated in the riots in our school to oust an overtly anti-Semitic professor, one Dr. Knickerbocker. The Joe McCarthy years blackened many good people, produced hosts of casualties, but for me it was different; indeed, it was the beginning of an exciting adventure.

The hotel was small, located one block away from the Place Capital, the center of the city, run with a warm hand, by a gracious concierge and his wife, Madame and Monsieur Lelang. They lived in a apartment on the ground floor, immediately behind the circular desk of the lobby.

The least expensive rooms were small, but opened to an

enclosed central court with a large circular skylight. I lived, uncomfortably, in one of these rooms. There was a sink, a bed, a large armoire with a full-size mirror, and a small desk. Like all the other students, I had a miniature kerosene burner on which to brew coffee, fry eggs, and cook hamburgers in a cast iron pan. Although my diet was Spartan, money being limited, given the inexpensive French bread, Camembert cheeses and wine, I made do with seventy dollars a month. The walls of this tiny room I decorated with paper blackboards, even the ceiling, and all the boards were covered with formulas and detailed drawings of nerve connections for my anatomy class. This room became my sanctuary—at once my library, dining room, sleeping quarters and a place to dream of someday becoming a doctor.

The concierge had no objections—at least none that he voiced—to my transformation of his room into an extension of the medical school.

Each morning a small elderly lady came to make the beds and sweep the best she could, especially the multi-colored chalk dust that covered the room and pervaded the air, inter-mingled with the odors of fried food, wine, and tobacco smoke from the night before. There was one large stained brown bathtub for each floor, for which we had to make reservations two days in advance. Weekends were the most desired reservations, and, of course, the hardest to get. Madame Lelang ran a fair game and could not be bribed by the richer students to get first crack at this marvelous luxury. She provided soap and large woolly bath towels for the sump-tuous and exhilarating experience. My room was moderately heated but the bathtub room was like a sauna.

Most of the students were considerably better off than I, financially, and they frequently took their meals at one of the

numerous nearby restaurants where the food was inexpensive but delicious. It was a luxury I could not afford. My fellow compatriots staying at the hotel included two rather
unattractive women on a Fulbright scholarship who had
come to learn French culture; one medical student from St.
Croix, whose name was Ralph; a man from Brooklyn,
Rosenberg by name, and Lionel Williams, from New York.

Rosenberg spoke French fluently because this was the
second year he was in Toulouse, preparing to retake the tests
which he had flunked the first time. When he opened his
room shutters, I could see a line of dried kosher salamis hanging in his open armoire. Each week they arrived, much like
the newspapers, promptly and without fail. Bringing salamis
to France is much like bringing a sandwich to the Cote
Basque Restaurant in New York. But this hardly concerned
Rosenberg. His room looked and smelled like a New York del-
icatessen when he fried his treasured salamis on his kerosene
stove. Salami and eggs—fit for the gods on Olympus, he
thought.

You could always tell Ralph, the St. Croix native, was near
by his cough. It echoed throughout the night because he kept
his shutters opened. Ralph, a mild and gentle man, also spoke
French fluently; he too was in his second year in Toulouse,
having also flunked his exams. He always had a cigarette in
his hand, holding it like Peter Lorre in the old movies, at the
center, between his thumb and index finger, raising his hand,
palm up, to meet his lips whenever he took a puff.

The oldest of the group was Lionel, a black man from
New York City who had a wife and two children living in
Harlem. All his life he had wanted to become a doctor. Now
with grown children, his wife had to remain in New York,
working hard and sending him money to enable him to pur-

sue and fulfill his dream. It was his first month here and he knew little, if any, French. He had been away from school for more than twenty years. Heavyset and tall, with a shiny face and a warm smile, Lionel was affable. He and I quickly became friends. We shared common bonds: New York, limited funds, little knowledge of French, and our first year in Toulouse. Lionel was a decent and generous man with a vision of a golden tomorrow.

At night, whenever he cooked meatballs and spaghetti, he always shared his meal with me. In the mornings, we left together for the bus at the Place Esquirole, which would take us to our destination and hopes, the ancient Toulouse medical school, with its long marble staircases and the anatomy laboratory which dated back centuries.

In November, after our first two months at the school, the dissections of human bodies were performed. Twelve rectangular slabs were covered with gray corpses, men and women. At first Lionel and I gasped with astonishment to see so many dead, and I could tell he was disturbed at the thought that they were about to be mutilated. Lionel was a deeply religious man. Each night before going to bed he read the Bible. Now, as he stood petrified, I saw him moved by his generous heart, offer a silent prayer. We were assigned to the same corpse— an Algerian who had died of gunshot wounds. There was an even hole in the center of his head, another in the chest. In all, four students were assigned to each corpse. Lionel and I were to start on the leg. We could not understand the instructions the professor raced through in French. A young assistant who spoke a little English gave us some basic directions about how to proceed with this ghastly business. The dissection kits were old and rusty. In college we had better tools for our frog and cat dissections. I held the scalpel in my hand, pointing at the skin. And then, for a second, I recalled the words of Macbeth: "Is this a dagger which I see before me,/ The handle toward my hand? Come, let me clutch thee/ I have thee not, and yet I see thee still."

The incision was made; the skin of the thigh was tough and resilient, as hard as leather. Fluid oozed out of the incision. The strong smell of formaldehyde made my eyes smart and tear. It is a smell I will never forget. These were old bodies, long frozen in the morgue, and then, thawing out, life came crawling out of the legs—millions of maggots swimming in the juices of decay. I felt faint, but the pungent odor somehow kept me from swooning.

"Clean the skin area and identify the arteries and nerves and carefully dissect them clean. Cut the main artery or nerve and you fail the course before it begins." Those were the discomforting words of Professor Rouviere, a tall, threatening-looking man with black hair pasted down on his head. The other students at our table knew no English. Two were Algerians, the other French. I marveled how adroitly they performed their task. Surely they were destined to be surgeons. The signs were there. How cool they seemed, while Lionel and I perspired. All of us wore heavy rubber aprons. The other two standing next to us were so confident that they seemed almost indifferent to what they where doing. How could anyone be so indifferent to human flesh? Wasn't this corpse once alive? What did the man do, what was he like? But now there was no name, just a number, 36660, and a gender designation, male—cold but efficient.

I watched the despair in Lionel's eyes. He was the same age as the corpse, the remains of a man who was now nothing more than a harbor and restaurant for maggots and an instrument of learning. I wondered—not for the first time—if this was the right profession for me. Carefully, we moved the fat to one side and, finding the long gray nerve, began to clean it. Pull too hard, allow the slimy scalpel to slip and that slender thread would be sliced through.

When we left in the darkness of the night, our bodies reeked with that smell of death, especially our hands. Once back in my room I quickly stripped off the offensive clothing, only to remember that there would be no washing machine, no bath to soak in. These clothes would remain my uniform. I'd have to live with the stench.

Sitting at my desk, the French anatomy text spread before me, written in French, I began the tedious task of translating into English; then came the memorization. Thousands of pages to memorize for just one course, and then all those others to follow—and all in French! Small wonder most flunk the exams the first time. How did anyone pass?

Becoming increasingly despondent, surrounded by the smells which almost made me retch, I heard a gentle knock on a door. So many sounds came from that busy courtyard that I wasn't sure if the knock was intended for me. This time of the night it could only be Lionel bringing me a cup of tea, as he sometimes did. Then we would sit and talk about New York and his family, and his eyes would become moist. He was so terribly lonely that first month. The knock came again, more insistent, and I knew it was not Lionel.

Standing there was an apparition, a vision. My first thought was that the fumes of the formaldehyde must have gone to my head. She was the most beautiful woman I had ever seen. She was sleek and bright-eyed, vivacious and animated. She spoke first—in a voice I found adorable—as she saw the astonished look on my face. She must have detected the stench of the formaldehyde, I thought, but she didn't make a comment about it.

"I saw your light on," she said in French. "Do you smoke?" she asked in English, her accent totally delightful.

"Yes. Please come in." The only chair in the room was covered with clothing.

I stuffed the clothes into the drawers of the large armoire that took up a good part of the room, and, rummaging around in there, found a pack of matches and handed them to her.

"You are an artist," she giggled, looking up at the ceiling covered with the anatomical drawings. I wanted to be surrounded by the names and the images so they would become as much a part of me as my arms and legs. The first thing I saw each morning was the arterial supply of the stomach as it was on the ceiling.

"No, I am a medical student."

"Yes, I heard you were the new one in the hotel."

Her perfume mingled with and then overcame the disgusting smell of the formaldehyde, or at least so it seemed to me.

"My name is Monique," she said, tilting her beautiful head slightly to the side. Her hair was brown and short, almost like a young boy's in prep school. She touched the side of her head and I saw that her fingernails were covered with a deep red polish.

"You are still studying," she said, "and it is so late. I will leave you to your work."

"No, no. I have had enough for tonight," I blurted. "Please."

I closed the door behind her and she came over to my desk and peered at the anatomy text.

"It is all in French," she said. "Do you read French, *un peu,* a little? I can help you, if you wish, in the evenings when you are back from your classes."

This was surely a dream.

Her body was small, slender, a perfect match for her delicate head and arms. Unself-conscious, she sat on the unmade bed, smiling and fully comfortable. After a moment, she rose, walked to the desk where I was sitting and leaned over me to peer at the book I still held.

"That is the *cuisse*, how you say?"

"Thigh, *Voila*, thigh. It is not pretty without the skin."

She laughed seductively, and I became weak.

"I will come tomorrow again, and I will help you translate."

"You don't have to go."

"Oh *oui*, it is late and I must get my beauty sleep." She kissed me on the cheek and left the room. For the rest of the night the room was filled with her perfume and I was filled with thoughts of her.

I touched the hair on my head and remembered these hands were covered with the stench of the dead.

In Europe, the students were an elite group, almost always forgiven for their wild ways. If they got drunk the Toulousian would say, "Oh, *c'est un etudiant*, they are students, what do you expect?"

You could always tell a student in Europe in those glorious days of the fifties. Most were unshaven or bearded, wearing old worn clothing. There was an air of freedom about them. No one was required to go to classes; all the learning was up to the student. There were no guides, no rules, only the final exams, the brutal task which always lay ahead, never for an instant out of mind. A one-time shot at the golden ring of success at the end of the year. Most repeated the year. Sometimes they stayed for several years to pass that first year.

Once the first was passed, the next seemed easy.

American students were even more special because of our reputation, often accurate, of being rich. I was an exception to the rule, and no one would quite believe I had barely enough money to eat more than one meal a day. It was almost impossible to have any social life without cash. I was prepared to lead a life of loneliness and celibacy and to concentrate all my energies on preparing for and passing the exams.

The second home for the students was the café, a welcomed reprieve from their small, dingy, usually cold and poorly-lit rooms. I went as often as I could to the café and nursed a cup of coffee for hours sometimes, undisturbed by any obsequious waiter. Here I heard French being spoken, and watched, with great envy, love at work. Smoke-filled cafés with students busily speaking, surrounded by young women, laughing, not paying much attention to an obvious-looking American. Then, when it looked hopeless to meet anyone, I walked the narrow streets at night back to my dreary hotel, through the foggy night. I was hopelessly in love with love. I carried a sweet melancholy in my soul.

All around me there was love. Even Rosenberg, the salami king, managed to have a girlfriend visit him. This hotel had such thin walls, especially the one in which I was interned, facing the court. All the sounds of the night entered the rooms. Ralph coughed all night, and Rosenberg's carnal grunts pervaded the court like a bad porno movie.

Too excited to sleep, I worked until dawn and finished memorizing the arteries and nerve supply to the leg.

Breakfast consisted, as almost always, of a cup of Nescafé, some French bread and butter, and a slice of Camembert. At five in the morning, most of the students were up and about, having already started their studies and continuing until it was time to catch the bus at eight.

Lionel was at my door at five-thirty, a walking corpse who was grinning affably.

"You had a guest at 1:00 a.m.," he said.

"Well, yes, a dream floated into my room," I told him.

For the rest of the day my thoughts were of Monique. At the lecture hall we sat on marble steps as the ambidextrous professor lectured on and drew the anatomy of the leg, using different colored chalks, one in each hand, to sketch in the arteries and the nerves. He used not a scrap of notes.

"Gentlemen, that is how you must know each inch of the body."

The lecture hall was half empty, which was hardly unusual since attendance was not required at any of the lectures, but only for work in the laboratories and the hospital.

Lionel was struggling to catch some of the words the professor spoke. The Toulousian speaks a special French, a wonderfully musical version. They also roll their R's, making it almost sound a bit like Italian.

With little sleep and being distracted by my fantasy of Monique, I heard little of the lecture, but once in the anatomy laboratory and at our post by the leg of the corpse, there was no time to daydream. Stress ruled. Lionel struggled fiercely with his dissection. I could see the frustration line his face.

Later we sat in the café sipping coffee; we were so exhausted that studying was simply not possible. The café on the Place de Capital was crowded with students smoking Gauloise cigarettes. I had a few packs of milder Phillip Morris cigarettes in my room that I dared not show in public. American cigarettes were a premium.

"It is awful hard for me," Lionel said. "I try to remember just a little, but my head is like a sieve. Everything falls out. I can hardly understand a word, much less memorize it all."

"Lionel, it will come. Tonight you and I will review the leg and then we'll go over the biochemistry, which I think I can manage to understand."

Supper was always the same for me—hamburger patty grilled on my hot plate, some cheese, lots of bread and a cup of Nescafé. I wanted some fresh vegetables, especially a tomato, but we had been sternly warned that tomatoes were a common source of TB. In 1952, this illness was the scourge of the medical students in Toulouse.

The hotel smelled like a cheap, greasy diner at dinner time. Lionel and I worked until eleven, but it became quickly and unhappily apparent to me that Lionel was simply not going to learn the voluminous material. He had been away from school for too long. His concentration was earnest, but ineffective. He looked so tired when he left my room that it broke my heart. His eyes, swollen and red, were set far back in his drained face, and he barely had the strength or will to speak. Everything had become a huge effort.

I made a schedule for myself to memorize and draw each section, a schedule corresponding to that of the professor. We had 8 months in which to learn all of the anatomy, 10,000 pages of memorization, and five other subjects before the examination in April. All in French.

At the stroke of midnight, there was a gentle knock on the door. Monique was standing there, dangling an unlit cigarette in her wondrously feminine hand.

"I have come to help you. You are not too tired?"

"I have been hoping you would come. I was going to knock on your door if you didn't."

Monique lived two rooms down the line. The shutters of her room were always tightly shut, but soft music came through the door, as did hints of her intoxicating perfume.

All over the bed and the chairs and the entire room I sprinkled Old Spice after-shave lotion, hoping to get rid of the ever-present smell of formaldehyde—at least to blunt some of its sharpness.

She wore a different dress and blouse and high heels, which made her shapely legs even more exciting.

We sat by the desk, she moving her delicate fingers over the page, translating the complicated language of medicine, occasionally pausing to turn her seductive brown eyes towards me with a smile, which only served to make her even more alluring. By one in the morning I could no longer restrain myself, and I kissed her cheek gently, as if I was afraid to damage the union.

"*Mais*, no. You have to study, *Cheri*," she reprimanded. "You are a poor student, aren't you? Not like the others?"

"Yes, but why do you ask?"

"*Comme ca*, like that."

She rose and disappeared again. I began to wonder if I hadn't really invented her. She appeared only at or shortly after midnight. For weeks after she had left, I stole past her room every night, using my trip to the common toilet as a pretext. No sound came from the room, no light from under her door. Sometimes I knocked softly on her door, knowing full well that the echo carried throughout the court. It was like announcing that I was in insatiable heat.

Studying was becoming more and more difficult; also, now I devoted more of my efforts to Lionel. We cooked together on his little stove, or, rather, I should say that he cooked all sorts of concoctions with sausages and lots of bread. Lionel began to change noticeably as the days passed into weeks, and the changes did not augur well. He couldn't remember the day of the week before stressful lessons, especially those dealing with the anatomy of the brain and all its highly complicated tracts and connections. I was managing, barely. I found the heart to be the most exciting organ, especially the marvelously intricate functional anatomy—or was it because I was a hopeless romantic?

"Lionel, 'the seat of the soul resides in the heart,' according to Aristotle," I said to him one night.

He laughed wearily and said, "That's not what the Bible says. God resides in all of man, in all of us, even we Negroes."

He had a small radio in his room, an ancient Zenith, and he listened to the Armed Forces' station that played good American jazz. When Louis Armstrong sang, he sang along with him—"I'll get by, as long as I have you . . . ," and he did a little tap dance to the music, trying to rouse himself. But he was so lonely and frustrated that tears came to his eyes. He was a shy and humble man who could have had many friends, but he considered himself just "another nigger," had convinced himself that the white folks truly didn't care for the likes of him. He wasn't wrong. The French were, outwardly, very tolerant to the blacks. Lionel found this amusing. He knew better. I could see the pain in his eyes when one of the students would casually ask him to turn his hand over so he could see if it was white on the surface of the palm—as in monkeys and apes. The student knew of the vicious attacks against the blacks in the South and knew all about the lynchings. They did make an extra effort to be kind, but it was cruelly condescending. They regarded blacks as poor, child-like victims.

One night, at the end of November, Lionel invited me to dine with him in one of the marvelous restaurants.

"You know, it's Thanksgiving in the States. We will have our own Thanksgiving here."

The other American students kept much to themselves and made their own plans. We found a small bistro on the Rue de Bourg, and for five dollars we could ill afford we had a delicious six-course meal. To keep some semblance of Thanksgiving tradition, we ordered *coc au vin*, the closest thing we could find on the menu to represent turkey. We drank a cheap Algerian wine. By the end of the dinner, we had both grown mellow and melancholy.

"You really miss your young lady," he said. "I see the sadness in your eyes. Man, you are young and good-looking. You will find dozens of others. It's a sure thing."

"Lionel, I know, but one needs time and some money." This beautiful young woman just up and disappeared out of my life. Embarrassment—or was it plain shyness?—prevented me from making any inquiries about her. I felt offended, hurt. My ego was shattered. I concluded that I just wasn't good enough for her. But the memory lingered.

In the weeks that followed, I could study little and waited for the night to come, hoping that there would soon be that gentle knock on my door which would relieve me of my misery, lift the weight of depression from me.

By the beginning of December I decided to get out a bit. There was a student restaurant which I decided to try. It was cold and raining, and I took the long walk to the medieval building through the dark, narrow streets of Toulouse. A pungent odor surrounded me from the sewage that flowed in the gutters.

The restaurant was crowded with French and Algerian students, all waiting in line with iron trays. I followed the line and took one of the unappetizing metal trays, along with a glass and worn silverware. Military style, they filled each section of the plate with French Fries, sausages and withered tomatoes, and filled the glass with Algerian table wine. At the cashiers I had to present an identity card, one which I never went to get at the bursar's office. Standing directly in back of me was a tall, scrawny-looking black woman holding her tray, stacked with double portions of vegetables, meat, and two glasses of wine.

"Oh, he is American. Let him go by. I will explain everything to him," she said in French. I got through.

"*Merci*," I said to her, grateful for her concern and kindness.

"Don't waste your time in French. I'm an American. Follow me and I will teach you the ropes."

There were miles of long wooden tables in this school cafeteria, with the haggard and exhausted students eating from their metal plates. The smells of food permeated the air, mixed with smoke—such dense smoke—and wine and unwashed bodies and clothes. There wasn't another American in sight, except for my new friend, Clarice.

She found her own spot and thrust her thin body on the bench, between two other students.

"If you don't push and shove, these frogs won't let you in," she said simply.

The scene looked like a movie I once saw, one starring George Raft at Alcatraz.

"So you came to join the Foreign Legion in Toulouse. You look like a bright kind. Why aren't you in Yale or some other spiffy joint?"

I didn't answer her.

"How long have you been here?" I asked.

"Five years," she said, "and I will stay until I pass my exams."

The French system of medical school consists of a five to six-year course. Two examinations are given, one at the end of two years, and then the final at the termination of the studies. The examination period itself takes months, involving ten to twelve exams. The student must get a passing grade in eighteen of the twenty exams. Otherwise, they have to repeat all the exams again the following year. Some students take ten years or more to pass their exams. Some give up. Some simply get too old to care.

"This is a good place to learn French," she said, "but you need a girlfriend to really learn the language. Do you have any money?"

"No."

"Too bad. That will make it very hard. With money, you get slides, a good skeleton, good English texts and even tutors. And, of course, you need money to take a woman for coffee."

"Do you have money?" I asked her.

"*C'est drol*, that is funny. Would I be eating in this prison cafeteria? I manage."

She wore a long nondescript dress. Her hair was unkempt, she looked shabby, but she burst with life and enthusiasm. Most of the students who passed us greeted her. I must have met a dozen of these in only a few minutes.

"Come home with me. I have a roommate you may like. She speaks no English, but you aren't a bad-looking guy."

We finished eating and left the cafeteria. We walked with long quick strides through the windy streets for almost an hour; then we reached a row of small houses.

"We live on the ground floor—two bedrooms, a kitchen, a small living room."

"Danielle!" she yelled. "We have a visitor."

Everywhere in the room were books and papers, most opened, strewn on the floor and on the kitchen table.

"I will make some coffee," she said. "Push them aside and

find a spot. I usually sit on the floor."

She continued speaking while she made the coffee, but I was unable to hear a word.

Danielle came into the room wearing a housecoat. The light in the room was dim, but I could see she had dark hair and was buxom, with large round eyes. She was not a particularly attractive woman, and she appeared considerably older than I.

"There you are, Danielle. Were you sleeping? This is our new friend, an American medical student. He has to learn French because he will never pass."

"Enchanté," she said.

We all sat on the floor drinking coffee, while Clarice chatted on, and then she suddenly rose and said, "I have to study and leave you two alone. Before you leave—when you leave—you can borrow my bones. I have a very good skull, femur, radius, pelvis, and hand. The rest you will have to scrounge around for. You have to learn each crease on the bones and holes in the skull and what goes through them. If you pass anatomy you are on your way. Most of the students flunk anatomy and biochemistry the first time around. Hope you do better."

To carry on a conversation with a total stranger without knowing the language is not without its difficulties. Danielle was able to follow some of my Enlgish, and we limped along. It grew late. Classes began at eight in the morning, and I wondered how I would get back.

There were no buses. Clarice solved my dilemma when she rejoined us.

"It's too late to go back to your hotel," she said. She must have read my thoughts. "Stay here and we can leave together in the morning. You can sleep with Danielle. She won't mind."

Clarice explained to Danielle, who simply said, "*d'accord*, all right."

Danielle's room was neat and organized. There was a cross on the wall and a wonderful painting of the Virgin Mary on her dresser. No books or magazines cluttered up her room. The night was chilly, and I was glad to be under the covers of the large down feather *duvet*. Soon she was beside me, while her robe was neatly folded over the chair.

It was good not to be alone, but all night I thought of Monique, even as we made love.

In the morning she served me *café au lait* in a large cup, and a croissant, while I was still in bed. Clarice yelled from the other room, "Get the hell out of bed. I never go to class before noon. I am only doing this for you. We have to catch the bus at the place Essquarole to make the first lecture."

By the look Danielle gave me as I left, I knew she understood I would not return.

In Toulouse, the week or so before Christmas, there were no signs that the holiday was fast approaching. Few decorations bedecked the stores; occasionally, a Christmas tree was visible. Christmas in France was a serious, somber religious holiday. After midnight, after church, all the restaurants and homes had a huge dinner, called *Le Reunion*. The Americans almost always took this time to go skiing or traveling so the hotel was almost empty. The concierge, Madame Lelang, was a kind woman and she had a large decorated tree in her living room.

"Monsieur is staying for the holidays?"

"Yes, it is better. It will give me a chance to do more studying."

She knew I was lying, because I was late by a week or two with the rent. I wasn't leaving because I was broke.

"Well, then, you must join us, if you have the time, of course."

Lionel cooked a small goose and sweet potatoes on his stove, and we listened to the Armed Forces network program that played Christmas carols all night. We drank champagne and wine and sang along. Christmas in Toulouse was hardly Christmas in Vermont.

After midnight, I staggered back to my room and fell asleep on my bed. I didn't hear the knock on the door, but felt a gentle kiss on my cheek and knew I was dreaming again. Monique stood above me, perfumed, lovely in a red dress. Only the light filtering in from the hall entered the small room.

"Merry Christmas, *cheri*," she said, and handed me a Christmas card and a large chocolate heart. But it was no dream when I pulled her towards me. I needed her to be real, genuine, nourishing. She was.

In the morning, without makeup, she looked even more beautiful than the night before.

"Where have you been all these months? I waited and waited, disturbed and even annoyed. If you had only written or called me."

"Well, you know. It was better this way. My father was ill, and I had to stay in the country with my parents. Let's be happy," she said, "and we must begin Christmas Day the French way."

She returned a few minutes later with a bottle of champagne, two glasses, real coffee, two croissants, and a small radio.

"We better stay home today. It is snowing too much."

In our rooms, night and day were one. Monique brought two blue candles, a miniature Christmas tree, a plastic reindeer in a glass, and a beautiful doll with brown hair. She owned a small turntable and a collection of Edith Piaf, Charles Trenet, Yves Montand, and Frank Sinatra. She transformed this small depressing room into a magic wonderland. It became night again. The flickering light of the candle reflected in the mirror of the armoire and made her silken skin glow with a maddening intensity.

We laughed and made love and slept, and ate delicious French cheeses, and drank more wine, and smoked Phillip Morris cigarettes.

When I felt hungry, she made an omelette of herbs. We ate chocolate and bread in bed. Sometimes my eyes wandered to the section on the ceiling where I had a blackboard mounted with biochemistry formulas. I strained to read the formulas in the candlelight. Monique made haste to prevent me from returning to reality by placing her small delicate hands over my eyes.

"*Mon petite chou*, there is time enough for your chemistry on the ceiling. There is enough here. *Fait le pratique sur mois*, practice on me."

We whispered like lovers, told of everything in our hearts while listening, enraptured, to Edith Piaf singing, "Mon Amour."

"From now on we speak only in French," she said, "and if you don't understand, *tampi*, too bad, your loss. You must learn French very well because you won't pass your exams."

An entire day and another night went by, and in the morning she left the room with all her lovely possessions, except for the doll with the brown hair.

"In case you forget about me, or you have another girlfriend, my *poupee* will remind you. See how her large brown eyes stare at you. Beware, *mon amour*."

I must confess that I had completely forgotten about Lionel, who must have surmised why I haven't surfaced for nearly two days. I knocked on his door and was surprised that he was not at his desk. He kept his room immaculate. He didn't want "the white folks to think we niggers are dirty." He used a pine spray in the room, lest there was the slightest chance of offending the cleaning lady. All our rooms were malodorous, reeking, but not his. His bed was made, the towels neatly folded, and there was nothing in the room except for his cooking utensils and some cans of food, neatly stacked, a bottle of wine, and a carton of Phillip Morris. His clothing was gone, and there was a note on the desk, and a large envelope addressed to me.

Dear Lover Boy:

    I did not want to disturb you, but I have to leave. I am too lonely and it is no use. I can't ever learn all of this stuff. I tried as you well know. I don't belong in medical school and will make out fine at home. You will be a great doctor someday, and I want to thank you for being so kind to an old man. Please take my oil cooker and food, and radio. The envelope is for you. When you get your M.D. and make good money, you can repay me. What use are French francs to me anyway? Take care of yourself. Peace and love.

Inside the envelope there was thirty thousand francs—about five hundred dollars!—enough money for me to finish off the year in luxury and to buy that needed skeleton.

My throat was dry, my eyes moist. Dear kind Lionel, my irreplaceable friend. I'll miss you, always.

Monique had disappeared again for two days, and when she returned late at night, she brought a little present, a "good luck pen."

"I didn't come to see you because you must study. It is very difficult to pass the exams here in France, you know, and I want to stay here with you, but if you do not succeed, I will be to blame."

"And if you don't come here, I will also fail because I cannot concentrate enough to study. So it is better you are here, and I will study like a mad fool, drawing energy from you." A smile and a pause. "Where do you disappear to? You are so mysterious."

"*Mon cheri*, mystery and longing is the secret of lasting love, so we say in French."

"Where do you go?" I asked her again.

"Oh, you know, I have parents I must stay with in the country, outside of Toulouse. We live in a vineyard, and my father makes wine. Someday, we will perhaps go together."

On week-ends, Monique became more generous with her time. Knowing we would soon see each other was the motivation I needed to work twice as hard and efficiently. We met often in the center of town, at the Place Capitale, in the Cafés des Artistes, where, apparently, Toulouse Lautrec had once come to do some paintings.

"It is better that those nosy people in the hotel don't see us together," she said. "*Je suis tres propre*, I am very morale, you know. In France, we keep our private lives very discreet."

It became apparent that Monique was no ordinary shop girl. She was educated, *au courant*, as the French say. She always looked as if she had just walked out of a stylish dress shop. Scarfs of colorful silk were as much a part of her as her beautiful brown hair. She was wearing a leather coat, a blue and brown scarf casually around her neck. It was becoming cold, and inside the café there was the smell of warm wine and cigarettes. She was sitting demurely by a small round table near the window. The late afternoon light made her beautiful hair shimmer. She was sipping on a cup of coffee, and just for a moment I wanted to look at her as from a distance, objectively. Her small lips were on the porcelain rim of the cup; one of her adorable fingers with the red polish rested on her chin; her legs were tightly crossed, her ankles touching. She must have just arrived because her cheeks were fresh and red as apples from the cold December air.

When I approached her, her face lit up, and she said, "*Tien, tien, mon petite chou*. Did you work well?"

"Very well. So well I have the day free."

"And the night?"

"Of course, the night." She gave me a tiny kiss on my cheek, and her eyes glowed with such love and passion that I wanted to smother her with kisses right then and there.

"What would you like today?" she asked.

"Are you serious? You need to ask?"

"My hungry, starving student. Good things are better if you have to wait a little for them, you know."

"I know, I know, only too well. I've waited a lot. Would you mind coming along with me. I have to buy a skeleton."

"*Mon Dieu*, he has gone crazy. I am not good enough for you. You need another one with no flesh."

We took the tram to the Rue de Metz, to one of the student's homes. He was an Algerian living in a small attic in a huge and ancient mansion. His room looked not unlike mine, and smelled as bad. When he saw Monique his eyes nearly popped from their sockets.

He wanted seventy dollars for the skeleton.

Monique said, in English, "Oh, no. That is too much for old bones. Tell him you have only forty dollars. He is poorer than you and he probably is making money on it. You don't know these Algerians like I do."

Right at that moment a bitter war was being fought in North Africa, the French Foreign Legion trying to subdue a revolt of the Algerians who demanded their independence.

Monique was right. He accepted forty dollars.

We put the skeleton in small shopping bags, and Monique carried the skull, which wouldn't fit.

"Is it a boy or girl?" she asked. "How can you tell?"

"If it starts rattling when you touch it, it is a boy," I said. "It's a girl. You can tell by the pelvis."

"Oh, *voila*, then I have to be a little jealous when you are alone at night with this slender mademoiselle."

We took the tram, staying close, our bodies touching as we held the skeleton. The French are blasé—or is it jaded?— even the bare head in her arms caused no stir. Part of the skeleton leg protruded from the bag, and this was accepted, too, but when the tram made a sudden halt and all the bones came flying out of the bag, it was simply too much, even for the French. The passengers gasped at the parts of the skeleton strewn all over the floor. It looked like children about to play pick up sticks.

We quickly gathered up the bones and got off the tram.

"Oh, he is a medical student," someone yelled, and they all laughed and envied us the way we looked at each other.

Love makes you feel confident, unafraid. It gives you the inner strength and security to make fun of everything, and makes you want to laugh at that which once seemed so terribly serious. Love gave me a sense of freedom I had never known. I could breathe again, drawing in huge and delicious gulps of clean air.

Now we were together most of the time. While I struggled nightly with the difficult task of learning, Monique stayed in my room. Languidly dozing on the bed or reading a book of poetry, she would catch my eye and wave to me as if she was in a distant field. Sometimes, she stole behind me and touched my head with her lips while her arms encircled my drooping shoulders. Slowly, I would turn my head and her face would be near mine. I followed the curve of her thin eyebrows and touched her small, curved nose to her lips.

"Not yet, *mon dieu*. Go back to your histology. There are only a few months left."

Like most of the other students, I stopped attending classes because there was just not enough time to do everything. The day began at five in the morning, Monique sleeping soundly while I brewed some Nescafé and worked until eight. Fatigue was one feeling I never felt now. So inspired, so driven was I, that grueling hours of study even became enjoyable. Learning is not usually fun, but I had my own private drive. *Everything* was fun. Carnal pleasures and scholarly endeavors, coexisted, side by side, each prompting and enhancing the other.

I was one of the lucky few, the recipient of those two treasured civilized gifts. When each cell of my brain was filled, overcharged, each synapse worn to the ground, Monique knew at once by my drooping eyes and planned a brief change to allow my brain to rest.

We took the train to visit the ruins in Arles, the old museums and buildings in Montepellier, and on one weekend we took the train to the Riviera.

Nice in the month of March was cold and windy. This great playground of the world now belonged to the people who made their home by the sea. The empty cafés looked like ghosts, and the hotels, even the famous Negassgo Hotel, was stark and awesome—a grand lady asleep, without makeup, but still elegant and beautiful. The stony beach which soon would be covered with beautiful people was now washed by the sea. The salt air cleared my brain. In just a few hours I was reborn, anxious to return to the job. Such wisdom in such a young woman. It was as if she herself had once endured the rigors of being a medical student.

As the days to the exams grew nearer, I became more nervous, even neurotic. In the middle of our lovemaking, I would jump up from the bed to check on something I thought I had forgotten.

"*Mon dieu*, of all the men in the world, I have to fall in love with a medical student," she said. Physical pleasures could not scotch my fears and anxiety. Nothing that Monique said or did could erase the accelerating madness in my brain, filled to overflowing with images of dancing arteries and nerve connections and complex and intricate formulas. My texts and I merged into one—a necessary but loveless marriage.

Now, in the final weeks, I saw Monique only once or twice a week.

Spring arrived, and the air was so fresh and gentle, the cafés were again alive, majestically lining the streets filled with young lovers. Late at night, when Monique was not with me, I would take a break from my studies and walk through the old narrow streets of centuries-old houses. The streets were charming, but many had a stench from the open sewers running through them. I would recite out loud whatever I had memorized that day. Onlookers simply took me for a madman. They nodded and moved on. Prostitutes of all sizes and shapes, young and old stood along these dark streets calling

"*Vien, cheri*, a little love in the night" which I found amusing; this was part of the charm of Toulouse.

Some of the faces looked familiar to me because they were required by law to check in the clinic each week to be tested for venereal diseases.

Their *carte d'identité* had to be signed stating they were free of disease otherwise they would be arrested by the police.

The medical students were assigned to their care which was part of the clinical training.

The final exams were like a lottery. Two subjects are picked from a hat, and these become the written portion. If a passing grade was achieved, then the student was eligible to take the oral examinations.

On the morning of the lottery the students gathered in the medieval courtyard of the medical school. It was a lovely morning, and there was a carnival atmosphere. The younger students, those who did not flunk the examinations the first time around, were kicking a soccer ball, others were smoking furiously pacing back and forth still high from the Maxidol they took the night before to cram for the examinations. Monique and I stood in the shadows of the old pillars of courtyard. She looked elegant and beautiful, her arm around me, my heart racing. Would I pass? It was impossible to know all the subjects in detail, especially the anatomy. Each student hoped painstakingly that the two subjects picked would be their strongest. My hopes focused on anatomy and biochemistry, or physiology.

One of the proctors, Bernard Bouley, from the anatomy laboratory was standing in the center of the circle of students, holding the traditional worn top hat containing white slips of paper, upon which, written in gold, were the names of each subject.

Outside of the circle, Monique pushed closer to my side, waiting for the chosen student to put a hand into the hat. A blond-haired student that I had never seen stepped smartly forward. He was apparently quite a popular man because they all shouted "*Alle, Alle,* Jean Paul, go, go, Jean Paul."

"You don't know him?" Monique asked. "He is very well liked. He was picked the king of the medical school ball this year."

I knew of the ball, but I hadn't had the money or the clothes to attend. Also, I didn't really care very much.

"It is histology and legal medicine," the blond boy shouted. Some of the students groaned with pain while others cheered. I was absolutely crestfallen because these were the subjects I had studied the least.

"Don't look so doomed," Monique said. "You have some weeks more before the exam and you can make a quick review, *n'est-ce pas?*"

The next three weeks were like a nightmare. I saw little of Monique.

"We must not drain any energy from you," she said. "I have a little present for you to make your brain better." She gave me a handful of vials with a green solution inside. It looked like something to put into a bath to make bubbles.

"It is glutamic acid. All the students use it. It makes you calm and helps you to memorize better."

Pharmacology was one of the subjects I studied, and I panicked. Had I already forgotten what I learned? I knew it was an amino acid, but I could not find it in the text. In one of the lectures the professor had mentioned it briefly. When she left I threw the vials in the wastebasket in frustration.

The Hotel Henri became one large study hall. None of us

slept very much. We crammed desperately, trying to digest everything written in our voluminous textbook. We formed small study groups with Rosenberg, Ralph and an Algerian student, and studied questions handed down by students who have gone before us. We had to know every crease on the bones of the body and skull, every formula, all the French laws pertaining to legal medical aspects of murder and genocide, euthanasia, homosexuality, perversion and drug abuse.

We were reviewing and mumbling to ourselves like a group of Jesuits reading their breviary in a monastery. Even those lucky few students who had superior memories had to keep their noses close to the grindstone. Our task was made even more difficult because, of course, it all had to be learned in French.

Some of the students relied on Maxidol, a drug which allowed them to stay awake and study all night.

During those grueling nights and days, Monique weaved in and out of the room, staying just long enough to be embraced. Most of the time I hardly noticed her, but her perfume filled the room; or she left some bread and cheese, or a paté or sausages or chocolates. My underclothes and socks were cleaned and folded neatly on the bed, and she left little notes:"*Mon petite chou*, work hard, I miss you."

The night before the examination the silence of the hotel was broken by dozens of young voices, shouting women speaking in English and laughing. Bearded, in my pajamas, I slipped out of my tiny room, and saw dozens of beautiful young women checking in and rushing up the narrow stairs to their rooms. Holiday On Ice, a British Ice Capades group, had checked into the hotel and were friendly and anxious to spend the evening with us. When I returned to my room expecting to see Monique, I saw instead a cute young blond sitting on my bed. She tried to entice me. Monique was so much more attractive and womanly. It took a lot of cajoling to have her leave. "Are you one of those funny chaps," she asked me.

"No, just in love with someone else and I have a examination to take in a few hours," I told her.

For the rest of the night there was laughter and singing throughout the hotel.

Sleep was impossible. It was nerve wracking to have this last important night sabotoged by the Ice Capade ladies.

Our group arrived at the examination hall bleary eyed and fearful. It was a written examination for both subjects and it was a miracle how sharp my brain functioned in spite of the raucous, sleepless, night before.

By the middle of May, it was over. Euphoria mixed with silent prayers and more sleepless nights while I waited for the results to be posted on the bulletin board of the medical school.

If I flunked, I half convinced myself that it mattered little to me as long as Monique was with me. This rationalization offered some relief from the strain. The word was out in the café at Place Capitale that the names of the successful candidates had been posted that morning. We rushed, like the insane, to the bulletin board, Monique holding and squeezing my icy hand. Some students came back cheering, others bemoaning fate—another year of torture.

Rosenberg came back smiling, and so did Ralph. Monique insisted that she look at the bulletin board.

"I will bring you good luck, my dearest."

I watched her trim body stretching to see the names, and she returned a few minutes later, silently, with not a trace of expression on her face.

"*Eh bien, mon doctor*, you passed!" she squealed and flung her arms around me and wouldn't stop kissing my teary eyes. We jumped and danced, squeezed until our ribs hurt.

Although it was only the first year, it was the essential test, even though the many years ahead would be as trying as this one. If I knew then what lay ahead of me, I doubt that I would have continued.

My euphoria was quickly dampened when I received a letter from the Board of Examiners in New York, signed by the commissioner of education (who would, in a few years, be removed from office for improper conduct).

Unfortunately, the state of New York Board of Examiners stated, a degree from a Toulouse medical school would no longer be acceptable in the U.S. I had to transfer to a medical school in Switzerland if my degree was to be transferable. Money had by now run out, and I would have to return to New York to work during the summer as a waiter in a summer resort in the Catskills. But none of that truly perturbed or disheartened me—except having to leave Monique.

Now, school over, we spent every precious moment together.

Everyone should be in love at least once in the spring. Old Toulouse became a garden of love. Miles of opened cafés packed with young and old, sitting, talking, eating, thinking, in the young sun of the new day. Women in large aprons scrubbed the sidewalks in front of their homes. The outside markets, a kaleidoscope of colorful tulips and daffodils, intermingled with the displays of hundreds of cheeses, sausages, breads, meats, and fish. Everywhere were the smells and whispers of spring. It was intoxicating.

Monique and I were like hundreds of others, holding hands, bending our heads together, always kissing each other, sharing those wonderful sweet secrets and glances only lovers know. And the laughter, which was as much a part of love as hugging, whispering and the endearing naughty and absolutely carnal thoughts.

My French was fluent now, thanks to Monique, and we rarely spoke in English. French was meant for making love; it is more romantic than any other language.

"I want to know everything about you," I told her, "what you looked like when you were a child, your family, all your secret thoughts and fantasies; yes, even about all your lovers."

"*Mon dieu*, this is too much. A French woman never speaks of her old lovers. You want to possess me like a *poupee*, like my doll. You let me keep a little of myself, young doctor-to-be. "

We were sitting on the concrete parapet facing the river, the Haute Garronee, that snakes through the burgundy country and down to the region of France, called the Midi. Men and women were there by the hundreds, their fishing poles in hand.

"I am jealous of your dreams," I told her. "Each smile you give to someone else is a loss for me."

"*Arrete, mon petit folle*, stop my little fool. That you have so little experience with women is obvious. Of course we love each other today, it is spring. But tomorrow, when the bloom is off the rose, who knows? When you return to New York, you may come back married."

"Never, you are the first love I have ever known, and I don't want anyone else. You'll see. Wait for me."

I wrote to Monique every night from New York. She was with me every minute in spirit. She answered in her delicate handwriting. I tried to contact Lionel, but he was no longer living at the address he gave me. All my letters were returned:

"address unknown."

I worked as a waiter at a hotel in the Catskill Mountains, and the summer passed. I was the classical obsequious waiter but it did not earn me more tips. "A medical student, everyone in the Catskills is a medical student," one miserable guest at the Napanach Country Club said to forewarn me that no larger tip was coming for having that distinction. I had earned just enough money to squeeze through the coming year. I had wanted to earn more so I could take Monique to Nice and buy her nice things.

October finally arrived. I had survived the misery of the summer knowing soon I would return to the country I learned to love and Monique. I missed "everything that flows in Paris" as Jean-Paul Sartre wrote. The smells and sounds and colors of Toulouse where with me each moment of the day. At least once a week a letter had arrived from Monique, but in the two weeks before I was preparing to leave for France, none arrived. Not hearing from her was agony.

Returning to Europe in October of 1952 was not an easy journey to make. Plane fare was very expensive and the Atlantic crossing by boat took five to six days. The Il de France, a grand ship, sailed at midnight from New York. I was on her.

In October, the sea becomes rough and exciting. I paced the decks like a wild caged animal as the winds howled, bent and raised this 44,500 ton ship as if she was a canoe. Soon, I would be seeing Monique, and neither a storm nor any power on earth was going to stop me. The Il de France made it safely home, and I disembarked filled with excitement and impatience. First, there was the train from Le Harvre to Paris, and then another train, the night train, the Oriental Express, Paris-Istanbul, to Toulouse.

At six in the morning I arrived in Toulouse. The taxi driver was a typical Toulousian, wearing a beret and singing his words. It felt good to converse in French again. The streets were empty, gray, sad-looking, and when we arrived at the Hotel Henri, there was one light on over the sign that read "Tourisme." My mouth was dry and I felt my heart pounding through my shirt.

Monsieur Lelang greeted me affectionately at the desk. He looked like he had just climbed out of his bed. Nothing had changed over the last few months. The straw chairs, the small center table, and the posters advertising the ski resorts in the Pyrennes on the side yellow wall were all in their same places.

My eyes rested on the narrow circular stairs that led to the second floor, where once I lived in my room of paradise.

"Does Monique have the same room?" I asked.

"No, she is no longer here, *Monsieur.*"

A sledgehammer hit my head.

"Where did she go?" I asked in panic. "Did she not leave a message? She knew when I was to arrive. I wrote her a dozen times."

"She was picked up by the police," he said quietly.

"The police? Monique? Are you sure? Why? What happened?"

"Eh *bien*, she did not go for a check-up and failed to register."

"Check up? What are you saying?"

"In France, all the *putaines* have to register, and a doctor exams them once a month."

"*Putaine*?" Monique a prostitute? Not possible. Are you mad?"

"Everyone knew it," Madame Lelang said. "We were sure

you did. We had warned her not to bother you, and we threatened to make her leave the hotel."

Madame Lelang saw my face, pale and perspiring, almost lifeless.

"Please sit, *Monsieur*. We really did not know you were not informed. She never told you, or asked you for money?"

"Of course not. She brought me presents. I never gave her anything. She said she visited her parents' vineyards, not far from here, when she was away."

"My poor man, you were so deceived," Madam Lelang said.

"I have to find her. I must see her. It is surely a mistake."

But it was not a mistake. The police had her registered as a whore, a call girl. After her mandatory medical check-up for venereal disease, she paid a small fine, was released and had not been seen again. That is why she had disappeared so suddenly. Everything she told me was a lie. She never once even hinted at her profession, and I had never seen her at the hospital clinic. Perhaps that was why she made love so magnificently—an artist at her craft. Does she tell such lies to all her customers? I really believed she loved me. Sometimes I wondered what she found so wonderful about a poor medical student when she was so beautiful and alluring.

I turned away from the desk because I felt sick, my stomach knotted. I was dead inside. Another part of my life was over. When I boarded the train again several hours later for Switzerland, I thought, for an instant, that I saw her in her leather coat, a colorful scarf flying in the breeze, walking arm in arm with a man with gray hair, leaving the station.

Perhaps.

Also available from Lorenzo Press

THE ROSSELLI CANTATA
by A. S. Maulucci

A novel inspired by the true story of a search for revenge that lasted 35 years and turned into forgiveness.

"Written with the strength and simplicity of a folk tale . . . Maulucci has a fine grasp of Italian American life."
—Eugene Mirabelli, author of *The World at Noon*

"Swiftly told, poetic prose . . . Maulucci has a gift for storytelling."
—*Voices in Italian Americana*

"A compelling new novel . . ."
—*The San Diego Union Tribune*

ADRIANA'S EYES AND OTHER STORIES
by Anthony Maulucci

Twelve stories of love, family and the search for identity. Some poignant portrayals of the Italian American experience.

"Stories are well crafted and deserve wider attention
. . . shouldn't be missed."
—*Primo Magazine*

"Natural storytelling skills . . . The Carpenter's Son'
shines like a gem."
—*Voices in Italian Americana (VIA)*

"Reminds us of why reading was so pleasurable a couple of decades ago . . . The essence of good stories by Hemingway and Cheever is recaptured by Maulucci in much the same way that a younger musician pays homage to John Coltrane or Miles Davis."
—James Coleman, *The Red Fox Review*

THE DISCOVERY OF LUMINOUS BEING,
a novel
by Anthony Maulucci

Set in Montreal during the Vietnam war, this is the story of one crucial week in the life of a young American man.

"We come away convinced that [the father and son] are flesh-and-blood people, and their issues are very much contemporary."
—Norm Goldman, *The Best Reviews*

"A highly lyrical, bittersweet, romantic story."
—Bill Brownstein, Montreal journalist

"Excellent work . . . The story has the quality of a Picasso line drawing."
—Herb Gerjuoy, *The Red Fox Review*

About the Author

Siegfried Kra, M.D., F.A.C.P. is an associate clinical professor of medicine at Yale School of Medicine. Author of numerous articles, textbooks and short fiction, Dr. Kra has also witten several medical books for the general reader including *Aging Myths* and *Is Surgery Necessary?* He is a contributor to the highly praised collection of essays, *A Piece of My Mind*, published by the Journal of the American Medical Association in 2004 and has had dozens of short stories published in *Medical Economics.* Dr. Kra has appeared on national television and given front-page interviews to newspapers across the U.S. *A Doctor's Visit* is his first book of fiction.